SHADOW STRIKE

THE FIRE WITCH CHRONICLES 2

R.A. LINDO

PERIUM PUBLISHING

CONTENTS

AUTHOR'S NOTE

The Fire Witch Chronicles is a spin-off series, following a character from the **Kaira Renn Series.**

There's no need to read the Kaira Renn Series, but please be aware there are some references to the original series.

WELCOME TO A MAGICAL UNIVERSE

Welcome to the secret, magical universe of **The S.P.M.A. (The Society for the Preservation of Magical Artefacts.)**

If you want to delve deeper into the magical universe of the S.P.M.A., **sign up** to become eligible for free books, private giveaways and early notification of new releases.

You can also join **my private Facebook group** where all things S.P.M.A. are discussed.

Founders' Quad Map

Society Square Map

A WAITING GAME

Merrymopes milkshake and ice cream parlour rests quietly in the evening light. We're preparing to start night duties on the trail of Neve Blin, the reason we're here instead of Pat's Caff — the usual meeting point for Night Rangers. Noah's got himself embroiled in another bet, throwing more Kyals at the likely hiding place of Neve Blin.

Rumour has it the ex Domitus is holed up in The Royisin Heights, blending into the underground world there with the help of a disfigurement charm. Conrad isn't arguing that Neve *isn't* there; his bet is that she won't be when we finally catch up with her.

I don't care either way and, thankfully, neither does Lucy, rolling her eyes at me as Noah and Conrad argue on the stake they're willing to bet, deciding on an arm wrestling contest to decide things. It looks like we're in for a long night.

The Merrymope twins who run the place are parked away on the upper floors of a building as colourful as its owners — red and white running along the walls and furniture. Like Pat's Caff, Merrymopes has normal hours and Night Ranger hours: a welcome dose of tranquillity for the exhausted society soldier.

The four of us sit in the private booth sectioned off from the main customer area, out of sight of prying eyes. Now, it's just a case of passing the time before duty calls, taking us to The Royisin Heights. With the arm wrestling in full swing, I study my Follygrin, hoping to catch sight of Neve Blin, but she's mastered whatever disguise she's using.

With no sign of the Domitus in hiding, I turn my attention to Lucy. She's been unusually quiet recently, probably due to her hidden feelings for Noah. Not as hidden as they once were after Zoe Tallis brought the first tinges of jealously to the fore. Lucy's pretty and funny but a bit of a mystery in the romantic realm of things.

I wasn't sure she even liked boys until Noah finally got a date with Zoe Tallis. We don't talk about 'the date' although that hasn't stopped us hanging out in Rebel's Rest which opens until the early hours. Noah does his best to ignore Zoe when we're there now, and the four of us avoid the topic altogether.

There's always something going on to keep us occupied, the current whereabouts of Neve Blin to current dilemma we're facing.

"You'll be out of Kyals soon, the way you're going on," Conrad comments, finally winning the arm wrestle.

"Getting cold feet?" Noah prompts, spinning his Vaspyl in his hand.

The Vaspyl transforms from a small, silver horse to a candle for our table: a nice touch improved by Lucy's utterance of 'Flori', adding flowers to the table.

"A romantic dinner for four," Noah jokes, drawing laughter from us all.

Conrad sits alongside me in the leather booth. I'm in my Night Ranger uniform of black leather trousers and top of the same colour. It's the look I adopted when people started calling me The Fire Witch. I like the name so stick to my all-black attire, adding a bit of style to our evening travels.

"So, you definitely want to bet we find Neve in The Royisin Heights?" Conrad asks again, concerned Noah's getting hooked on betting at every opportunity.

"Yep. Where else is she going to go?"

"Anywhere she can hide," Lucy counters, tapping her feet on the red-and-white striped floor.

"Then place your bets," Noah encourages, brushing his floppy fringe away from his eyes.

"I can't take any more money off you; it's embarrassing," Lucy teases.

"I'll take the bet," Conrad agrees, "but only if you don't sulk when I win."

"*Deal*," Noah says with a smile, offering a handshake before he locks Conrad in another arm wrestle, the friends adding a touch of magic with the flight charm — flowers wrapping around their hands that lift them off their feet.

Lucy rolls her eyes, trying to hide the fact her attention's on Noah. He's clearly the boy she wants and with Zoe Tallis out of picture, she might just get her chance. She laughs at the sight of Conrad and Noah spinning in mid-air together, holding hands as if they're perfecting a dance: an arm wrestle turning into a comedy act. Neve Blin returns to my thoughts as the morning light falls over Society Square.

My money's on her staying put in The Royisin Heights, probably regretting her choice of tempting us into a duel. Friendly duels are okay but our little fire fight in Drandok wasn't of the friendly kind. No doubt, Neve will have another surprise in store when we finally track her down.

WITH CONRAD AND NOAH OVER THEIR MID-AIR WRESTLING match, we prepare to leave Merrymopes for The Royisin Heights. No door is needed to make this journey this morning, Merrymopes offering its own unique Perium to all Society realms. I place my penchant bracelet on the brass edge of the booth we're sitting in, listening to the bell ringing on the counter.

It rings of its own accord again, causing the entire room to shudder as the red-and-white leather booth descends through the gap beneath our feet. Once we get lower, we see the familiar sight of a large, circular room revolving at speed.

The only other thing in the room is the brass barrier framing it, stopping people from getting injured when they mistime their jump. The Revolving Room is another wonder of the S.P.M.A., a unique Perium accessible to the chosen few.

I used it a lot in my early days when being an underage witch was more of a problem. Then, it was advisable to travel unseen, particularly if I wasn't in the company of adults which was always the aim. Secret travel isn't required now but I still like the thrill of certain Periums: The Revolving Room being one them.

The fun is in jumping on and staying on, the room spinning so quickly it's easy to mistime your jump and be sent flying. There's a way of slowing the room down, though, which is what Conrad does now by placing his penchant ring on the iron dock we're standing on.

We time our jump as the spinning structure gathers speed, making our way to the middle where a brass dial waits to transport us to our destination. Instead of doing this, we stay on longer than needed, laughing as the room tilts and throws us off balance. The Fixilia charm takes care of this, freezing us to the spot.

"The first person to move buys the Jysyn Juice tonight," Conrad prompts, causing us to lock into Night Ranger mode: intense and still as The Revolving Room clatters in the surrounding space. We all remain perfectly still until The Revolving Room jolts suddenly, throwing Noah forwards with a yell of frustration.

"*Every time!*" he shouts, referring to his streak of bad luck on recent bets.

He can drown his sorrows with Jysyn Juice later. We've got an ex Domitus in hiding to track down.

"Let's go," I say, as we deactivate our Fixilia charms.

I reach for the brass dial in the centre of the spinning structure, dialling the required letters. Seconds later, the expected image forms in one of the doorways — the signal to move towards it and jump through: Night Rangers on a mission to tie up loose ends.

2

EVENING FLIGHT

We enter the strange stillness of The Royisin Heights, the endless mounds of earth a reminder of the reclusive nature of the people living here. Each mound houses a Society member within, the inside far more interesting than the outer shell. Sianna Folly-grin proved this when she appeared barefoot and detached, waving us towards her home near the peak of the rolling hills.

We've returned to a similar spot, hoping other things will be revealed to us ... most importantly, how to access the underground world hidden beneath our feet. Something tells me a Cympgus won't work but I try it anyway, uttering 'Whereabouts' to release a ball of blue light from my penchant bracelet.

The light does what I expect, floating through the evening light before resting on the surface of the hillside. Normally, the light would form into a shape, providing a portable Perium to our chosen destination, but nothing happens ... the faint, blue ball of light stretching out to form a zig zag line ahead of us.

"Maybe we should try to get Sianna's attention," Noah suggests, adjusting the waistcoat he always wears over his T-shirt.

"She's come here for peace and quiet," Conrad replies, "probably only helping us last time to stop us hanging around and annoying her."

"We could do with her wall of broken glass now," Lucy comments. "The way it penetrates secret places."

I doubt Sianna's going to make another appearance, keeping on my guard with the Vaspyl in my right hand — ready to activate the morphing steel into my favourite weapon if necessary: two swords for unwanted company.

There's no company around, though, just the faint light provided by the stars, highlighting how vast this realm is: endless silhouetted mounds of earth bursting through the surface, hiding reclusive witches and wizards who're probably watching our every move. There's no history of the inhabitants posing any sort of threat although that doesn't mean you drop your guard.

Anything's possible in this magical world of wonder, so the four us stay close together, Conrad alongside me as I raise my right arm, firing out a streak of blue light that stretches towards the stars. Without the power of portable Periums, we're going to need another form of magic to unlock the underground world where Neve is said to be hiding: a unique type of magic lacing the feathers of the Williynx.

Conrad, Lucy and Noah join me — the four of us standing in a circle, sending multi coloured streaks of light into the air, signalling for help from our feathered friends. Wherever they are, they'll appear through a Perium in the sky soon, releasing feathers towards us. Williynx feathers are blessed with unique magic, something we're going to need to continue our journey here.

"Why don't we just light up the ground, seeing if it marks out the underground area?" Conrad suggests, his impatience getting the better of him.

We agree on lighting up the *sky* instead of the hills, conscious of not creating any unnecessary problems. Sianna Follygrin was kind to us because she recognised two of us. Other inhabitants might not be, so we decide to decorate the sky with creative charms while we wait for our Williynx to arrive. The Canva charm is one of the first spells you learn: a simple charm allowing you to create any picture you can image.

The sky is our chosen canvas so I start things off with an image of a roaring dragon, filling the dark sky before letting out a silent roar as it powers towards. Lucy adds a gladiator to the moving light show, creating a David and Goliath scene as the small gladiator blocks the dragon's fire with her shield.

Ever the comedian, Noah adds a group of professors running away from the dragon's fire, their hands waving manically as the fire catches their robes. At the sight of our Williynx appearing in the starlit sky, I add a lighthouse: a symbol of the help arriving. Our feathered friends touch down alongside moments later, ready to unlock the world beneath our feet.

I pat Laieya as she lowers her head to the hillside we're on, using her sixth sense to pinpoint the space we need to access. With a mild squawk, my trusted Williynx rises a few inches from the ground, opening her wings to release a flurry of feathers. The feathers rest on the hillside, beginning the light show we really need: the outline of the underground world Neve Blin's likely hiding out.

All we've got to do now is wait for Laieya's feathers to work their magic, turning soil and grass into an access point, leading us into the busy ballroom hidden beneath, and an ex Domitus who's probably expecting company.

LAIEYA IS JOINED BY HER FEATHERED COMPANIONS, ALL hovering inches above the ground, releasing their own flurry of feathers. After a few seconds, the hoped-for portal of light appears, allowing us to enter without being seen.

An Invisilis charm sorts out most situations requiring invisibility, but everything about The Royisin Heights suggests a certain way of doing things. Portable Periums don't work and no witch or wizard comes out to greet you, meaning we're operating under different conditions.

Thankfully, Laieya and her feathered friends know what these conditions are, forming four perfect circles of coloured feathers on the hillside: fire-red, powder-blue, purple and yellow all morphing into lines of bright light as they touch the grass. With the circles in place, our Williynx touch down on the hillside again, lowering their heads in a signal for us to step into our own circle of colour.

"I think they want us to kneel," Lucy says through the spinning mass of yellow light surrounding her.

"Then what?" Conrad asks, doing as Lucy suggests.

"Then we sink through the soil in a blaze of light," I reply, adopting the kneeling position required.

JUST AS LUCY SUGGESTS, WE SINK THROUGH THE SOIL SECONDS after in our spinning circles of light. I'm a little uneasy about what we're heading into, keeping my Vaspyl in my right hand just in case. If it's what I think it's going to be, we'll be suspended in the air, looking down on the underground realm of The Royisin Heights, the light around us keeping us hidden.

How this works doesn't matter; it just needs to otherwise we'll be crashing into the crowds below. Society members who don't want to be found aren't going to hang around to be caught, meaning caution is necessary as we sink lower, the soft blue glow flickering around me fading away as I hover, suspended in mid-air.

Whether Neve's here or not isn't the immediate concern ... getting down from here is ... although how that happens is yet to be worked out. Noah just shrugs in his typically casual way, readying his defences just in case we can be seen — but it's the sight of Lucy, maintaining her kneeling position, that confirms we remain invisible.

Lucy hovers closer to the crowds than the rest of us, peering down to inspect the disguises worn by many of them. The disfigurement disguise is the one problem we've got, making it more difficult to know if Neve is hiding out here or not.

The Williynx's brilliant stroke of magic will help us with that though, our in-flight perspective allowing us to move around the ballroom, hovering over unfamiliar faces distorted by potions bought at the counters lining the underground lair.

We can't hang in the air all night so need to formulate a plan, not knowing if our voices are shielded from the crowds below. It's either going to be an exciting night or an uneventful one.

"Where are you hiding, Neve?" I whisper, deciding to

have some fun when I realise tapping my feet lowers my position.

Hovering above the head of a snoring wizard, I float around the ballroom, signalling for the others to do the same. Something tells me Neve's here but not in plain sight, meaning it's time to investigate where the ballroom leads to. The others work out how to move around in mid-air, tapping their feet to move left and right until we're close together again.

"What about a disfigurement charm of our own?" Noah whispers, confident we can't be heard.

This gets an immediate shake of the head from Conrad.

"Too obvious. It won't disguise our age."

"Then what? I'd rather be in Rebel's Rest or asleep like the old dude in the corner."

"We wait for a sign," I say.

"Helpful," Noah quips with a forced smile.

"What're you thinking, Guppy?" Lucy asks, following my gaze towards a group of woman who leave the ballroom, heading through the exit to our right.

"I say we find the toilets."

"The *toilets?*" Conrad queries.

"Not to go in them, but to check who's coming in and out of them. Disguises are going to be checked in the toilets," I explain, "particularly if you're a nervous Society member on the run."

"Clever, Guppy," Noah offers, jigging up and down like he needs the toilet.

"Looks like Noah's volunteered for the job," Conrad jokes, nodding at his friend's constant mid-air movement.

"Let's find out where they are and see if a certain Domitus appears, worried about her appearance. Come on, let's go before we blow our cover."

Tapping our feet together, we float above the ballroom crowds, checking disfigured faces as we go. So far, there's no sign of Neve who's either perfected her disguise or mastered the art of operating in plain sight.

She'll trip up, particularly if we reveal ourselves, unable to pass up the chance of inflicting some pain of her own. I doubt it'll be another duel, but it won't be a dance either so we float towards the exit, ready to find out if we've got another battle on our hands.

3

DOMITUS IN DISGUISE

We reach the ballroom exit, realising we're either going to have to reveal ourselves or trust the disguise our Williynx have provided. We need to go lower to get through the door leading out of the busy ballroom, but doing this means we're bound to make contact with the heads of comrades moving in various cliques of comfort.

Alternatively, we can just hope our blanket of colour lets us float through all solid surfaces, including the wall surrounding the door.

"I'm not a fan of embarrassing myself," Lucy states, looking like she's ready to utter 'Undilum' to deactivate the charm. "Let's just use the Disira charm to get us to the toilets. That way, no one sees us here and we make an unexpected appearance where Neve's most likely to be."

"You're forgetting she'll be in disguise," I challenge, "so the element of surprise won't help us unless we've got time to detect her in the crowds."

"Guppy's right," Conrad adds, tapping his left foot to slow our direction of travel. "There's no point revealing ourselves if it means Neve spots us and makes a swift exit or, worse, strikes out, dragging us into another battle. We're already getting a reputation so let's trust that our Williynx's magic can get us through this wall, leading us to whatever's beyond it."

"And if we end up head-butting the wall?" Noah asks with a sarcastic smile.

"Then all will be revealed," I reply, kneeling as we approach the whitewashed wall that changes colour the closer we get — a patchwork of light reflecting our protective bubbles. A few faces turn in the crowded ballroom, inspecting the shimmering fields of colour on the wall near the exit, but there's nothing more to see than a faint glow, fading moments after we're through — our Williynx coming to the rescue again.

Once past the exit, we're faced with iron stairs that spiral upwards. The staircases twist and turn as far as the eye can see, making me wonder how *underground* this part of The Royisin Heights is. It's no big surprise because the interior of most magical buildings is much bigger than suggested by the building it's housed within.

"Great. Another maze," Noah whispers as I tap my right foot hover higher, kneeling again so my head doesn't bang on the ceiling or take me back to the hillside.

Society members are crammed onto the iron staircases, some sitting in discomfort as their disguise takes hold with others scampering upwards, glancing back to make sure no-one's following them.

"I say we get to the first walkway and replace our Williynx' cover with a Verum Veras charm," Conrad suggests, bumping into my blanket of powder-blue light as a rowdy crowd tumbles down the staircase to our left.

"They look like they've had a few remedies too many,"

Lucy comments as we stay as low as possible, floating along the iron staircase to our right, our heads inches from the wooden ceiling.

"So, are we in agreement?" Conrad prompts, keen to get back on his feet to finish the job we're here to do.

We all nod, kneeling together as our protective bubbles gather pace, illuminating the figures who fill the staircases below — my attention on a figure ahead who moves suddenly at the sight of us.

I point to the second walkway to our right, adding, "*There*. Dressed in the blue coat with peacock flowers on the collar, pushing past the crowds as she climbs higher."

"Are you sure, Guppy?" Conrad asks.

"It's Neve and she's setting a trap."

"But she can't see us?" Lucy queries.

"She's obviously used a surveillance device to track our journey here," I reply. "Also, who's to say there isn't a remedy available here, allowing the user to penetrate invisibility charms?"

"It makes sense," Noah agrees. "People use this place as a hideout, meaning the remedies on offer do more than disfigure."

"Sort of like Crilliun eye drops," Lucy adds, "but instead of seeing in the dark, you can see through all disguises."

"Allowing them to recognise the people they trust here," Conrad adds as everyone gets the gist of what I'm saying.

How else could you work out who anyone else was? The disfigurement disguise lasts as long as required, assuming you drink the relevant remedy, so the idea there are remedies to penetrate these disguises makes perfect sense — as does a remedy to detect people entering the underground world by stealth, like us.

As we float towards the second floor walkway Neve Blin has vacated, I add one more thing:

"The move was staged, making herself stand out on the second floor landing. The way she threw her coat over her face ... completely unnecessary if her disguise protects her from detection."

"So, it's a ploy to draw us in?" Conrad adds.

"Yep, so it looks like we're in for another dance."

"So let's dance," Noah says, clicking his fingers and uttering 'Undilum' as we reach a gap on the second-floor walkway — a passageway of iron stretching off in all directions.

We all follow suit, replacing our Williynx's initial protection with a more familiar blanket of invisibility: the Verum Veras charm. With our feet firmly on the ground, we stand together within a glimmering curtain of multi-coloured light, about to track an old foe to her hideout.

———

THE CROWDS LESSEN AS WE GO HIGHER, TAKING THE ROUTE Neve Blin used to disappear into the darkness. Flames light the higher walkways, flickering as we move along a narrow archway marked with indecipherable scribblings.

I get a shiver of recollection when I glance at the strange writing, hoping it isn't another secret code forming in a hideout the Society elders largely leave alone. I hope the only malev in hiding at the moment is the one we're tracking, meaning The Royisin Heights can be left in peace.

"Quivvens," Conrad whispers as we walk along the passageway illuminated by soft flames.

My Quivven's already buried underneath my heart, glowing a soft blue as we close in our target. Whatever

Neve's got in store for us won't change her fate, meaning she's likely to strike out the moment we're in range. Time for the wizarding games to begin. As the passageway veers off in both directions, we separate ... Lucy and Noah taking the right passageway with Conrad and me veering left.

I've got the feeling Neve isn't alone up here so I ready my weapons: two swords and a shield of shimmering blue light, courtesy of the Promesiun charm. Conrad uses the Weveris charm to extinguish the flames lighting the passageway, using the small, black webs to throw us into darkness — our Quivvens will do the rest.

The art of fighting blind was mastered in the last war, closing our eyes to activate the Quivven's ability to map our terrain.

"She's here," Conrad whispers as we move slowly along the dark passageway, echoes of voices reaching us before a loud heckle fills the space.

It's not Neve's voice and I imagine it's a trick she's employing to wrong foot us, the Acousi charm generating whatever voice is required. Conrad has formed his Promesiun charm into two whips, the Infernisi charm circling around his feet as he moves. Flames will rise the moment any form of attack reaches him, incinerating objects or enemies trying to penetrate the circle of light around his feet.

We're used to strange locations for battle so ready ourselves for another dance with Neve. The first sound of combat comes from the passageway to our right, vibrations filling the space as Lucy and Noah pivot and fire back, the shimmering circles of the Infernisi charm forming a protective barrier as a cloud of black smoke swarms them.

They're prepared for all eventualities, using the Weveris charm to protect their noses, mouths and ears, the covering of ears in preparation for mind-bending creatures flooding out of a Zombul. Our Quivvens light up the space, allowing us to see Lucy and Noah's position through the wall of earth that separates us.

If Neve thinks we're trapped she's mistaken. Like Sianna's wall of broken glass, we can see every aspect of our surroundings — a privilege she's relinquished at the first use of a curse: no Society penchant responding to her call now. She comes into view seconds later ... holed up in an alcove high above us.

Lucy and Noah have already worked this out, activating the Velinis charm to surround themselves with another protective curtain of light. It just needs a co-ordinated strike to bring her down, and we've got just the light show to finish her little uprising.

"We send a flood of Ameedis her way and follow it with fire," I suggest, getting a nod from Conrad who keeps the whips of light and energy at the ready. "She obviously wants us to use the flight charm to get closer to her, which would be suicide."

"We're safer on the ground," Conrad adds, agreeing with the plan.

As another loud heckle rings through the space, we hear the first flood of voices closing in ... the sound of reinforcements rather than a mad rush of malevs, suggesting the secretive nature of this place isn't being used to form another cloud of darkness.

The battle isn't over yet so that assumption is put on hold. Our Verum Veras charms remain active, limiting Neve's ability to have clear sight of us. Whatever the remedy used to penetrate invisibility charms, it's limited by the blasts of counter fire she's dealing with now ... still seemingly alone in her alcove in the air.

Conrad whips his two lines of light and energy along the floor, before sending them skyward, twisting his body in the circles of protective fire as he shatters the floating alcove holding Neve. She's smart enough to jump off seconds before her platform explodes, activating another one as she does so.

Conrad's worked out her rhythm now, whipping his Promesiun charm at the Zombuls in both of her hands — her only weapon to force our submission. Curses and creatures controlled through a steel artefact aren't the same as the real thing swarming you, suggesting Neve's fall from grace is rooted more in bitterness than bad blood.

Grief has become her enemy, screaming at the sight of a flood of disfigured faces filling the exploding walls of earth. It looks like another blaze of counter fire won't be needed, turning to see a Society force behind me, arms raised towards the raging figure of Neve Blin.

"Fire and ice," whispers a familiar voice, and I turn to see Farraday standing alongside me: a permanently disfigured legend who's found his way to The Royisin Heights — about to do what he does best, ending uprisings with a spectacular light show. "Thought I'd come and say hello," he offers with a smile, nudging me and Conrad to get ready. "We send a line of light around Neve, drawing the frame of her downfall."

"And then?" Conrad asks, hoping for something a little more dramatic.

"Then we have some fun," Farraday replies as he nods to the collective following his lead. "Fire for the fallen!" he orders to the gathering of sleeping soldiers, and the light show begins.

4

FADING FIRE

Conrad and I decide to follow Noah and Lucy's lead, uttering 'Velinis' to activate a bubble of protective light around us. Although we have the Quivvens to map our surroundings, it's still unclear if Neve is dancing on moving alcoves alone here, so extra precaution is taken.

Defending our magical world alongside Farraday is always a blast — a legend who's officially stepped down from Society duty, now spending more time travelling through the S.P.M.A. or maybe something else.

Either way, I'm pleased he's here orchestrating the co-ordinated fire directed at Neve. She continues to jump through the air, generating new foundations each time she does, but it's only a matter of time before she has to adapt her strategy. There's only so much room in this narrow space, meaning the more crowded it gets, the less chance she's got.

I catch another glimpse of Noah and Lucy who spin and pivot in their protective bubbles of light ... Lucy deciding water might flush Neve out ... the Levenan charm activated to send a flood towards the perilous position of an ex Domitus who continues to dance in mid-air.

"She'll try to return to the surface soon enough," Farraday says, casually countering Neve's fire. "When she does, use the Entrinias charm to follow her."

"The Entrinias charm can transport us through the mud walls?" Conrad asks. "Like the Williynx did with their feathers?"

Farraday nods — the scars on his face and hands less distinct through the glow of the Quivven's light. "Yes. It can't get you in but it can get you out. Hidden places are always harder to access than leave."

"She's trying now," I add, deciding to activate the 'Propellus Celiri', lifting me into the air.

I judged this move to be suicide when it was just the four of us, but now we've got Farraday's army with us, offering greater firepower. As the stem of a daisy wraps around my right hand, I stay protected within the Velinis charm, rising higher which causes Farraday to call "HALT" to the co-ordinated fire.

The small Society army deactivate their blazes of light, watching as I float towards the cursed smoke flooding the air ... Conrad, Noah and Lucy rising with me as a bitter smile crosses Neve's face. Before long, every sleeping soldier present will lift off the ground, some activating the flight charm whilst others vanish in mid-flight, hoping to catch Neve before she disappears into the wilderness of The Royisin Heights.

I don't think she's planning on running anymore. She wants her day with us: the Night Ranger crew who've exposed her darker tendencies. She'll try to draw us into a trap but I've got other ideas, ready to come face-to-face with a creature tamer who's hidden venom has got the better of her.

As Neve utters the Entrinias charm to fade into the mud walls, I signal for the others to pause their flight. We're safe within our protective bubbles of light but this is only temporary protection.

Curses crack the surface of simple protective charms so we need to reappear on the hillside with a different strategy. Neve will expect us to step into a makeshift taming cell of her own making, meaning subtle movements are needed now.

"The Disira charm to get to the surface, reforming the Velinis charm when we get there," I say.

"I say we stay invisible," Noah challenges, floating towards the mud ceiling. "We don't know what curse she's going to use when she sees us."

"She's using a remedy to penetrate invisibility charms, remember," Conrad adds. "She knew we'd arrived the moment we floated down through the earth."

"Looks like we're going to have a little battle on the hillside," Lucy comments, "just when I was starting to think things were getting dull."

"I wouldn't call being flooded with curses dull," Noah adds as we prepare to follow Farraday in a vanishing act.

"Always so dramatic, Noah," Lucy teases, our eyes still closed with our Quivvens glowing under our skin, providing a shimmering image of what lay beyond — and a malev in the making outlining the space of her last stand with streaks of bright light.

"What's she doing?" Noah asks, pushing the mop of black hair away from his eyes.

"Preparing her last request," I reply before adding, "Come on, it's time to put our reflexes to the test."

IT TURNS OUT THE LIGHT NEVE'S USED TO OUTLINE HER LAST stand is the Infernisi charm: a ring of light turning into a circle of fire on contact. The ring of light is surrounded by the group of sleeping soldiers who, until Neve's performance, were minding their own business in a ballroom of remedies and disguises.

Now, they're lining the hillside of The Royisin Heights, preparing to take down a fallen comrade, but Neve isn't surrendering yet. Farraday maintains calm on the edge of the circle, controlling the steady hands of Society members keen to get back to their secret hideout, but duty comes first in all things, meaning putting the finishing touches to a dance that started in Drandok.

The four of us appear near Farraday, reactivating our Velinis charms until we work out Neve's plan. The silence on the hills won't last long, that's for sure, so it's time to put a new threat to rest. The circle of light erupts into flames each time a sleeping soldier tries to cross it: a sign that our ex Domitus only wants a certain crowd to join her.

Farraday steps towards the erupting flames, uttering 'Levenan' to surround himself in a tornado of water as he does. The water protects him from the flames, allowing him to enter the circle: a scarred hero who's dealt with far worse than a few flames and a witch with a chip on her shoulder.

"Time's up, Neve," Farraday says, keeping to the edge of the inner circle of light, knowing only too well the destructive power of curses. "Any use of Gorrah spells the end."

"I'm authorised to use dark magic," Neve spits back, spinning at every movement outside the circle. She's a witch on edge, all right. "I'm a *Domitus*. An authorised creature tamer with a permit to practice dark magic to tame deadly enemies."

"The only problem is, Neve, you're the enemy now."

Farraday's dressed in his usual uniform of black trousers, matching shirt and brown waistcoat. He isn't the force he once was but senses Neve's fading fire.

"You're turning your back on your own to protect *them*," Neve shouts, pointing at Conrad, Lucy, Noah and me. "*Children* influencing more and more of the Society after *centuries* of laws banning such a practice. *Children* being taught in faculties already making mistakes above ground, and *I'm the enemy*?"

"Children are rarely born to darkness; they acquire it," comes a familiar voice to my right: Sianna Follygrin ... dressed in a floral coat and winter boots, replacing the dressing gown from our first visit.

Neve turns at the sound of Sianna's voice, letting out a loud cackle. "*Sianna Follygrin,* offering wisdom after running for the hills. A Society living in blissful ignorance *again,* believing peace means opening the floodgates to fera*l* species and untrained minds.

Look at you all, hiding up here or living in the comfort of Society Square, letting resentment build. Your new world of bliss is creating problems you can't see — problems you *won't* see until The Velynx is full and you ask the *right* question."

"And what would that question be, Neve?" Farraday asks, stepping closer to her as shadows form in the sky.

"Why so many throughout The Society Sphere are secretly seething, wondering how a glorious, magical universe has given into the demands of the young simply because they fought in a war and survived. Demands that will create divisions once more.

Your talk of unity is as hollow as the gesture of creature taming — both forms of wishful thinking to those of you who live in comfort. You can't tame underworld creatures any more than you can create endless harmony, so get ready for the flames to rise again in places you rarely travel to?

Flames that won't stop by putting me and a hundred more in The Velynx. The very army you'll need when your vision of bliss and harmony collapses around your ears. Release me and I'll offer you the path you need to appease the growing resentment."

"Spoken like a desperate Domitus," I finally add, sick of her posturing. "If there's a hundred comrades like you, we'll find them."

"You overestimate your firepower, Miss Grayling."

"Well, let's find out shall we?" I reply as Conrad copies Farraday's trick of using the Levenan charm to access the inner circle.

I've already worked out this isn't necessary; the circle of Neve's last stand has been designed for us. It's a way for her to get revenge in any way possible. I doubt anyone present believes we're bullies who go around intimidating people, but there's a simple way to prove it.

We step into a circle of light and fire, ready to put on a display for the reclusive inhabitants who appear out of their homes carved into the earth.

"Hold your fire unless otherwise stated," Farraday orders, deciding to stay in the circle to referee proceedings. "Society soldiers choose their battles: children and adults alike."

No response comes from the gathered crowd who look on ... arms placed uneasily by their sides ... ready to fire out protective and defensive charms if things go haywire. I recognise very few of them, even with their disfigurement disguises fading on the hillside. If Neve's right and resentment is growing at the idea of children in the S.P.M.A., it's time for us to remind them of our loyalty to the cause.

I stand next to Conrad with Noah and Lucy flanking us. There are no creatures this time so fury will be released by our imaginations, and I already know how to prove who the real villain is. With our Quivvens glowing under our skin, we begin the dance to end a Domitus' lie. Subtle movements to force a reaction from the opposition ... no one having activated a charm of any kind yet.

In close company, battle is like a poker game, giving your opponent nothing that can be used against you. It's exactly what Jacob is teaching his class through the Rucklz tournaments on The Hallowed Lawn: the critical ability to *react* and *adapt*. It won't be long before Neve is forced into making her move, sensing the presence of creatures in the starlit sky: winged comrades ready to descend should they be needed.

We wait in the middle of the circle for the emotionless malev to make a mistake, which finally comes when a wave of sky urchins storm down from the sky — their speed enough to shock a questionable comrade into action.

"*Now,*" I say, kneeling as I throw my Vaspyl into the air, transforming it into a set of iron bars, signalling where Neve's heading: the cells in The Velynx.

Between the sight of the steel bars floating towards her and the Silverbacks Noah's made from his own Vaspyl, our emotionless target is caught between blasting our creations out of sight and preparing for the sky urchins' attack. Her choice is an obvious one, glancing at Farraday for help that isn't forthcoming ... before a Fora charm is used to halt the sky urchins' charge.

Neve should know better but her panic has caused her

first mistake, thinking a protective forcefield is enough to stop the inevitable. Sky urchins are able to form Periums by parting the atmosphere with their hands, meaning they can vanish in and out of realms in seconds — a skill on full display when they re-appear in the circle of light and fire, hovering above Neve's head, holding off their attack to draw out the venom hidden inside our creature-taming comrade.

The final scene of submission is set as the gathered crowds enter the circle, surrounding themselves with water as they cross the threshold of fire.

"Prove yourself or suffer the consequences," Sianna Follygrin commands, raising her arms in the flood of water surrounding her, as if she's about to release it onto the comrade damaged to the point of darkness.

With the sky urchins closing in, circling inches above Neve's frightened face, she sinks to the ground with her arms over her face, spinning moments later to explode cursed fire at her accusers. The response is swift and majestic, the collective Society forces generating a huge walled web that divides the circle: a web that halts the curse, leaving us to watch the sky urchins swarm.

5

REBEL'S REST

The return to Rebel's Rest has its own drama, Farraday creating the Cympgus to transport us back to a calmer environment. As always, other sleeping soldiers deal with the transport of fallen figures, meaning the sky urchins will organise Neve's trip to The Velynx.

Her comment on the secret seething of some Society members has got me thinking, wondering how many people have got a problem with the youngest members of the S.P.M.A. If they have, they don't show it when we appear.

For me, the idea of trouble brewing was Neve's way of trying to escape her fate, which doesn't mean we can ignore it. Farraday had a little chat before we left, using the Telynin charm to squeeze the truth out before Neve was transported to The Velynx.

He'll tell us more when we get to The Singing Quarter, seeming as keen as we are to inject some fun into the evening. Being a Society soldier can be intense, to say the least, making the down time more valuable — and down-time's always a blast in Rebel's Rest.

With his failed date with Zoe leaving a sting, I half expect Noah to cry off at the suggestion, but he's the first to step through the portable Perium Farraday's created: a floating curtain of orange light. As Lucy vanishes through the Cympgus, I take Conrad's hand, daring him to run straight through instead of stepping in slowly.

The thing about Cympgus' is you never know what mode of transport you're going to get. Portable Periums make up their own mind, meaning it's more fun to run towards it, having to adapt to whatever happens next. Ever the competitor, I let go of Conrad's hand, laughing at the look on his face as I race towards the floating curtain of light.

"*Cheating!*" he calls, closing the distance between us before he leaps into the air, literally *flying* through the entrance to the Cympgus which is when the fun begins.

What's waiting for us inside is a rare form of travel: a shimmering, twisting pole of light stretching out ahead of us. I grab onto the pole, glimpsing Noah and Lucy whizzing along the line of light which dips and climbs in the darkness.

Conrad's desperate to catch up, hating the idea of losing, but he's going to struggle now I'm attached to our magical mode of transport, swinging my legs around the pole to get the maximum amount of fun out of the ride.

I fly through the darkness, letting out a yell as the pole twists into a sudden drop — the outline of a glimmering curtain below to halt the fall of the less experienced. The safety net might be needed as I feel Conrad closing in on me, facing forward with his legs wrapped around the pole. He looks like a racing driver closing in on his nearest rival, determination written all over his face.

He smiles as he closes in, waving to rub in the fact that

he's not going to be last, after all — or at least that's what he thinks. The only way he can pass is to let go when the pole twists upwards again, using his sky riding skills to reattach himself ahead of me. I know that handsome face too well, sensing when he's going to make his jump ... just as we reach the highest point of the ride.

"Cheaters never prosper," he whispers behind me, letting go seconds later with a smile that falters the moment he feels my hand on his leg.

Cheating's not my plan, *intimacy* is so I grab onto Conrad's legs as I let go of the pole, sending us into a sudden descent towards glimmering safety net. Night Ranging has taken us away from each other recently so I want to remind him of our morning sky dances, entangled as we fall through the air with our Williynx ready to scoop us to safety.

We've got a safety net instead of feathered companions this time, sneaking in a kiss as we hit the web at the bottom.

"Always over the top," Noah teases as we join the others by the shimmering archways of light, leading to our destination.

Noah holds out his arms towards Conrad, gently mocking our romantic moment in the air. "*Come on*," he teases, puckering his lips as he goes in for a hug.

He gets a headlock instead, the two friends play fighting as Farraday reaches for the outline of a lamp, pulling the string to spin us into the noise of Rebel's Rest.

"Jysyn Juice on you, remember for moving first in The Revolving Room," Conrad comments, nudging Noah at the sight of Zoe Tallis.

Noah doesn't take the bait this time, standing calmly at the bar with none of the desperation he once had. It looks like he's over Zoe or he's hiding it well: a sight that brings a smile to Lucy's face.

I point out our Rebel Crew to Farraday — the three friends who can always be found at this time of night, keen to get away from serious Society business: Jalem, Ilina and Harvey. Ilina's her usual elegant self, dressed in a purple coat and sequinned dress with a hat to match. Jalem and Harvey haven't gone to the same effort, their clothes and hair covered in colourful powders after a day in The Feleecian: the faculty for remedies.

Rebel's Rest is as rowdy as ever, a dance breaking out as another popular song fills the ironically titled 'rest rooms'.

Harvey gives out the hugs as he always does. "Capture any *baddies*?" he asks, pretending to fire out defensive charms.

"We ended a little argument," I reply, smiling at the friend who never stops moving, making me wonder how he ever gets any work done in The Feleecian.

"Who?" Jalem asks, all angles and bones in his powder-covered clothes.

"Neve Blin," Ilina replies over the noise of Rebel's Rest. "The table next to us were discussing it when we got here."

"Really?" Harvey queries, still jigging up and down.

"Do you two ever listen to a thing that's said?"

"What?" Jalem jokes, saluting Farraday as the scarred legend sits with us.

Not all scars heal, even with magical remedies like Srynx Serum, although Farraday carries his war wounds like a true warrior. Grabbing his glass of Liqin, he claps along to *No*

Witch or Wizard Knows: our table singing along except for Noah.

We'd normally be standing on the table by now, getting into the spirit of things, but Noah's brooding at the table — a certain date still on his mind. He might be over Zoe Tallis but still seems bitter about the way she led him on. Zoe's as confusing as Lucy but I know who I prefer: my Night Ranger girl who's as loyal as they come.

Luckily, Farraday doesn't do self-pity, banging his glass on the table as he leans closer to Noah. "If a scarred soldier can make the most of things, so can a Night Ranger," he states, slamming his glass on the table again to get Noah's full attention.

It looks like Farraday's about to lesson Noah in the reality of loss, leading me to stand from the table, gesturing for Conrad to join me.

"Come on, handsome. Let's move those dancing feet."

Conrad hates dancing but realises it's a way for Farraday to deliver his wisdom.

"I thought you'd never ask," he jokes as we join the groups dancing between the tables.

Jalem, Harvey and Ilina get into the rhythm of things as well, belting out the lyrics to *No Witch or Wizard Knows* as they stand on their chairs, leaving Noah to brood and Lucy to become more distant. Farraday grows impatient with the two of them, throwing his glass into the air and shouting 'Disineris'. I know this trick well, exploding glass to make a point.

The first trick I learnt was the ability to destroy and rebuild, which is what Farraday's teaching Noah now, using it as a metaphor for moving on. The Fora charm follows, stopping the glass as it falls ... the spinning glass forming a perfect circle over us ... a Spintz charm adding the final touch: a shattered chandelier for friends and comrades.

"Everything breaks in the end, my friend," Farraday explains to Noah, "so you have to focus on healing." He claps his hands before adding, 'More Liqin before we get onto our dance in The Royisin Heights."

I knew his appearance wasn't random, meaning we'll be here until the early hours, discussing the strange scribblings on the walls and the rumblings of resentment in other realms.

We've got singing and dancing to do first, though, and two sad friends to cheer up: Lucy sitting alone and Noah forcing a smile at Jalem's terrible robot dance.

Something tells me Lucy's *never* going to make her move, so I kick Noah into action.

"Bloody cheer up, will you," I say as empty drinks trays float across the rest rooms, finding their way to the bar.

"I'm getting tired," Noah complains.

"You're getting *boring.*"

"I'm just not in the mood, Guppy"

"When are you going to see that Zoe's *not into you*, and that someone else is?"

"What?"

"Guppy ..." Conrad's comments, signalling caution but I've had enough of treading lightly. It's time to kick Noah into action and sort this Lucy / Zoe thing out.

"Someone else likes me?" Noah queries, his expression changing from sadness to surprise.

"*Yes,* you idiot!"

"Who?"

I kick him again.

"*Okay.* I'm being miserable and stupid."

"So, *get over yourself* and see what's staring you in the face."

"Which is what?" Noah asks, looking genuinely puzzled.

"Maybe listen to Farraday's words," Conrad suggests. "You know, to focus on healing."

With Noah puzzling over Farraday's cryptic clue, Lucy gets up from the table. She waves goodbye as she moves towards the wood-panelled walls, reaching for the string on the nearest lampshade to transport her home.

"No you don't," I call, signalling for her to hold on.

"I'll leave you to the fun tonight," Lucy comments.

"Hang on for one dance, Lucy."

"I *can't*," she says, her pretty pixie looks flushed with sadness.

"You *can. Just take a chance.* How else are you going to know how Noah feels about you?"

Ilina joins us, leaving Harvey and Jalem to their strange dance routines. Taking Lucy by the arm, Ilina spins her into action. "If he doesn't dance with you, we'll make him vanish."

Lucy laughs as Ilina leads her towards Noah, adding, "All yours, lover boy."

Noah hesitates for a second before his natural charm returns, bowing comically to invite Lucy to dance. It looks like she's taken my advice to heart, guiding Noah's hand to her waist: a girl about to find a soulmate or heartbreak. At least we've done our best.

"Nice work," Conrad whispers, pulling me towards him.

More drinks trays fly through the air as the lights in Rebel's Rest go out: a sign to drink up and make our way home. Farraday's keen to share his intel on The Royisin Heights though, leaving time for a final round of drinks and one more slow dance.

6

RUMOURS & RUMBLINGS

We sit in the dim light of Rebel's Rest, glancing at the mess left by those who made a quick exit, certain to return for another evening of magic and madness. With the proprietors leaving us to our own devices, we share stories of our recent adventures with Jalem, Ilina and Harvey who love to hear about our exploits.

They're not cut out to be Society soldiers, preferring safer sanctuaries. They enjoy our stories though, Harvey taking on the role of action hero as our take down of Olin and Neve Blin is described.

Tiredness gets the better of our friends eventually, and they leave with a comical goodbye, Harvey forming a Cympgus which he pretends to fall through, grabbing Jalem and Ilina as they vanish through the glimmering tunnel of light together.

With our friends returning to the Feleecian, grabbing some sleep before they return to another day of concocting new remedies, Farraday turns to the question of rumblings and resentments: the point Neve was keen to make before the sky urchins decided it was time to shut her up. With his scarred hands tapping his empty glass, he looks out over the empty streets of The Singing Quarter, momentarily lost in thought.

Part of me wonders if he's thinking of his days as a Society soldier with Smyck: his close friend and oldest ally who died in the last war. He *must* miss that time when he could blend into any crowd, keeping an eye on malevs and black market rats. It's not as easy to do this now — the scars covering his body making him stand out a mile off.

That's probably why he likes the underground section of The Royisin Heights, feeling at home with witches and wizards in hiding, using disfigurement disguises to stay under the radar. Either way, it's good to spend time with a man who's saved my life more than once.

"Our old friend Neve didn't do her homework," he says, returning his attention to our table — the thinning, dark hair helping to cover the scars on the side of his face. "If she had, she'd have known that all Society realms have sleeping soldiers embedded in their fabric. We don't let anything slip these days, keen to avoid minor dramas developing into unnecessary problems."

"So, you're one of the sleeping soldiers in The Royisin Heights?" Lucy asks, looking a little brighter now she's finally got up close and personal with Noah.

All they need now is a date in The Winter Quarter, testing the strength of their love on The Sinking Bridge. Their first time together on the bridge was the fallout of another date with a certain someone Noah's trying to move on from, helped by a few kicks from me. I'm sure he'll thank me eventually.

"I'm one of them," Farraday says in reply to Lucy's question. "The other one was fast asleep when you got there ... the long-haired fellow with his head on the table. He thought it would be a good idea to mix aspirin with a few strong remedies, hoping to get rid of his splitting headache. Only made the headache worse until he started banging his head on the table, eventually knocking himself out."

"Not much of a soldier then," I joke, sharing a laugh with the others.

"The remedies there do more than temporary disfigurement; they help with pain."

"You're still suffering?" Conrad comments, wondering if he's over stepped the mark.

Farraday isn't the sensitive kind, though, rolling up his sleeves to show the bulging veins under his scarred arms. "A moving pain that never leaves me, due to traces of curses Srynx Serum can't heal. The price you pay for cuddling up with danger."

Our legendary comrade's dark humour refers to the lethal fragment he transported to its final resting place. He hates sympathy and self-pity — the reason he worked to snap Noah out of his sombre mood earlier. Anything can happen in love and war, Farraday once told me, so if you're going to step onto either stage, be prepared for the potential fallout.

"So, you weren't there to track Neve Blin?" I query, reaching for the drinks tray on the table next to us and throwing it in the air. It floats across the room, resting on the bar.

"Not exactly," Farraday replies, "but it didn't hurt that I happened to be there."

His smile lets me know it's more complicated than that, suggesting he hasn't completely relinquished his role as a sleeping solider.

"What do you make of Neve talking about people resenting us?" Conrad adds, throwing his empty glass into the air, wanting to see if it will float like the trays do: it doesn't. Deciding it's more fun to keep it spinning in mid-air, Conrad listens as Farraday offers more on the rumblings of resentment among certain Society folk.

"Neve's always been dramatic; I wouldn't read too much into what she said."

"But she meant it," Lucy challenges, tapping her fingers on the table. "It seemed genuine to me."

"Yes, it was," Farraday agrees, "which doesn't mean it was *accurate*, Lucy. The idea that some Society elders don't like the influence and access the young have isn't a surprise. Some of them still think *I'm* young.

There will always be sticklers for tradition, whinging about 'how it was back when', but that's par for the course. We're not talking about another uprising, as Neve suggested."

"It would still be good to find out where these rumblings are, though," Noah suggests. "Maybe see if we can put people's minds at rest."

"You're not the issue, Noah," Farraday replies. "Your Night Ranger crew, I mean. You've held firm to the principles of the S.P.M.A. — beauty and unity — enjoying the beauty and working hard to build bonds wherever you go. Yes, there's the odd 'intervention' but that's the role of Night Rangers."

"Noah's right, though," I add. "It would be better to meet the groups who don't trust us, ironing out any issues they've got with us."

"As I said, Guppy, their issues aren't with you."

"Who then?"

"Others of your kind."

"Other Night Rangers?" Conrad asks, glancing up at his floating glass.

Farraday nods.

"Who?" Lucy prompts.

"Have a wild guess: an arrogant crew who wear their Night Ranger status like a sheriff's badge, bursting in heavy handed without justification."

"Taeia's crew," Noah states, getting a nod from Farraday.

"Yes. I'd keep an eye on Taeia if I were you — within and beyond The Society Sphere — because if anyone's going to cause us problems, it's going to be him."

"Power mad?" I suggest, already knowing this about the handsome boy with a hollow heart.

"Status driven, definitely," Farraday clarifies, "and there's nothing wrong with that until it gets out of hand."

He turns to me when he says this, knowing I know exactly where a thirst for power can lead, currently to a twisted building on the margins of The Society Sphere where mum hides out alone: a fallen witch resigned to a life of isolation and judgement.

"So, what have Taeia and his crew been up to?" Conrad asks as a familiar intensity takes hold.

I'm one step ahead, whispering 'Comeuppance' as I take a Panorilum out of my trouser pocket. "Let's find out," I say, throwing the book into the air.

We watch it fold open, forming into a large piece of parchment paper: a surveillance device offering unique insight into our endless, magical universe.

"I always knew he was creepy," Lucy adds as we focus on the moving illustration filling our surveillance device, studying a group of Night Rangers storming into The Shallows with unnecessary force.

It makes me wonder if the appearance of Odin and Neve a while back was less about us than what we represent: young Society soldiers accelerated to positions of authority others have never reached. *I'd* be angry if all Night Rangers acted the way Taeia's lot were, strutting through Poridian Parlour like they own the place.

———

AFTER HAVING ENOUGH OF WATCHING TAEIA'S CREW throwing their weight around, we formulate a plan with Farraday's guidance.

"So, should we track Taeia or try to heal wounds?" I ask as the dawn light washes over The Singing Quarter.

"I'd ease my way into the realms they've offended first," Farraday replies. "I'll deal with the resentments in The Royisin Heights. Make Zilom your focus, working on smoothing things over."

"The land of suspended rain," Noah comments.

"And take a trusted guide with you."

"Who?" Lucy asks.

"Kerevenn ... our ageing giant who offered passage to Sad Souls when we most needed it."

"Why Kerevenn?" Conrad prompts.

"Because, like his kind, there's a lack of trust within certain Society factions: Night Rangers being the current issue. Your reputation precedes you so you'll be made to feel welcome. Kerevenn's also forged a path there, using his skill in healing to help wizards with fragile minds."

"I didn't know he travelled to Zilom," I comment, struggling with the first wave of fatigue.

"Mystery will always be an element of the S.P.M.A., Guppy, a central part of its magic. Not everything can or should be known, allowing people to make their own way within the bounds of peace and discovery."

That comment makes me think of the indecipherable

marks on the walls in The Royisin Heights, decorating the passageways leading away from the underground realm. Farraday doesn't mention them and, for some reason, I decide not to ask the question. I get the feeling the marks are part of a bigger picture — one about to unfold as we prepare to head to another realm.

"So, Zilom then Taeia," Lucy confirms, nudging Noah to keep him awake.

I imagine she's got more than nudging on her mind, frowning as Noah starts snoring.

"Looks like Captain Sunshine needs his bed," Farraday jokes as we stand together, thankful to be returning to the peace of magical faculties to get some well needed sleep.

———

WE WAIT FOR KEREVENN NEAR THE SEATING STATION, expecting the ageing giant to appear on the ground floor of The Cendryll in the early hours. His gentle manner and knowledge of all things magical impresses everyone, including the Society elders who've got used to seeing Ulux and sky urchins roaming the faculty for charms

With Yoran, the wise sky urchin who also hangs out on the ground floor, Kerevenn helps Jacob's class solve magical puzzles as they call their favourite Quij to gather books needed to complete tasks.

The Fateful Eight strive to impress, fully aware that a permanent place in the S.P.M.A. need to be earned. It will ultimately be Jacob's decision who isn't a fan of authority, evident in the way he wears his Society tie — the only compromise he's made regarding teachers' uniform.

He's got a parental way about him, appearing on the spiral staircase now, holding a cup of something to kick start his morning. A group of Quij flutter around him — the tiny, luminous insects drawn to my brother's energy, eventually returning to the task of collecting books from the shelves beneath the large skylight.

The Cendryll has been home to me for a while now, always feeling more like home when Conrad and Jacob are nearby. We'll catch up before he heads off to another day of teaching, apparently ready to take his students to The Glass Arch: the perfect training ground for young witches and wizards. Kerevenn tends to be an early riser, meaning he should appear soon.

Casper and Philomeena Renn control the room leading to Kerevenn's private quarters: a room full of boxes which vanish when the right combination's entered. Another touch of magic happens then, the frame housing the boxes vanishing as it falls to the floor, turning into a grid of illuminated squares, forming a spacewalk beneath The Cendryll's skylight.

The rooms at the other end are where Kerevenn spends his evenings, conditioned to isolation after decades in his original home of Sad Souls. The ageing giant is happier now — happy to be finally accepted in a world that once marginalised him: a Ulux who carries the name of his kind with pride.

Farraday didn't exactly say Kerevenn *would* help, but it looks like he'll be travelling with us to Zilom: a wise guide showing us the way in the land of suspended rain.

7

THE MIDNIGHT GUIDE

J acob makes his way over to us, raising a hand to familiar faces as the skylight washes The Cendryll with a soft glow. He looks a little more alert this morning, probably helped by the remedy he's sipping from a silver cup.

Conrad and I sit on the edge of the circular Seating Station, situated near the lift. It's a popular meeting place for witches and wizards, discussing the progress of new charms they're cooking up behind the doors lining the five floors.

In the past, discussions would have centred around the drama reported in *No News is Good News*, the Society pamphlet that litters the ground floor. In times of peace, the pamphlet is blank as it is now, offering no interest to Cendryll members who live for the unique thrills only magic can offer.

I push a blank pamphlet around with my right foot as Jacob sits alongside us, running a hand through his shoulder-length dark hair. At least he's combed it this morning, not something he normally bothers with.

"How are things in the mad, bad world of Night Ranging?" Jacob jokes, sipping the yellow remedy.

This particular brew is Liqin: the remedy for hallucinations. It's usually used after a run in with creatures like the Mantzils who occupy Quibbs Causeway — the pathway leading to The Velynx that anyone in their right mind tries to avoid. I imagine Jacob's chosen remedy is linked to the demands of teaching.

"Are they still driving you mad?" I ask, referring to Jacob's class known as The Fateful Eight.

It's the name given to the classes offered a unique opportunity to prove their magical worth.

"They're a bit frenetic," Jacob replies, sipping his Liqin as Yoran flutters towards us — the elderly sky urchin who's become a feature of The Cendryll.

"A clear day for fireworks," Yoran offers with a smile, adjusting the black rags over his scarred body.

Like the other sky urchins here, Yoran has refused to abandon his black rags, arguing that it's a reminder of the essence of sky urchins: soldiers destined for sacrifice. The Orium Circle — who make all the laws — tried to persuade the sky urchins of the benefit of new clothing, but Yoran argued a suit wouldn't hide their emaciated features or the scars on their faces.

It wasn't like they were ever going above ground, so suitable dress didn't matter: *tradition* did. So, black rags it is, meaning on a good day you can have Quij, Williynx and sky urchins floating in The Cendryll — a perfect image of wonder to pass the time.

"Fireworks?" Conrad queries, shaking Yoran's hand.

"We're moving on to the practical application of charms," Jacob explains, raising his eyebrows as he takes a big gulp of the Liqin remedy.

"The Glass Arch?" I ask, remembering the brilliant days I had with Kaira, Jacob and Farraday, learning how to smash the place into a million pieces before reforming it.

Jacob turns the palm of his left hand upwards, rubbing the ring on his other hand to call a group of Quij. He's got a habit of doing this when he's preoccupied or welcoming a nervous member to The Cendryll. He's the nervous one this morning, obviously worried about the chaos that's about to unfold.

"We can hang around if you like," I suggest. "It might help to have another pair of hands."

"Likewise," Yoran adds, offering a wise smile to an elderly lady who walks past nervously. Not everyone's used to scar ravaged creatures in the heart of the S.P.M.A.

Jacob smiles as a small group of Quij rest in the palm of his hand, their delicate wings fluttering. "That would be good. If you've got the time, that is."

"I've always got time for my big brother," I offer with a smile, my right foot still moving the blank Society pamphlet on the floor, part of me wondering if the suspicions surrounding certain Night Rangers will make the front page soon.

"We can keep an eye on Ethan and Lucy, making sure they don't blow each other up," Conrad jokes, turning up the collar of his black coat.

"And I can protect those who lose control of their charms," Yoran adds, his bald head shining under the soft glow flooding in through the skylight.

Jacob studies the Quij who buzz gently in the palm of his hand, their bright glow a permanent reminder of the wonder all around us. "The students don't know we're heading to The Glass Arch, or that we're practising more advanced charms, so expect chaos."

"Chaos is what we live for, big brother," I reply, patting Jacob on the shoulder.

"Chaos that almost got us killed more than once."

"But here we are, sitting in the heart of The Cendryll, mini legends with a story our old above-ground friends would *die* to tell."

"Mini legends...?"

"Well, *tiny* legends then, but you get my point. What's life without a little drama?"

"Peaceful."

"Boring," Conrad adds, going along with the mild humour.

"Minimal chance of being ripped to pieces by a Silver-back," Jacob continues.

"They're harmless," I joke, "They barely left a scratch on us in Drandok. You've just got to know how to talk to them."

"So, changing the subject, is everything sorted with Odin and Neve now? No issues with any other Domitus?"

"All sorted," Conrad adds, "although Neve said something that's got us thinking."

"Which?"

"The behaviour of other Night Rangers and the resentment it's causing: Taeia's crew."

As Jacob's expression clouds over, Kerevenn appears on the spiral staircase: the ageing giant who will explain more, hopefully agreeing to be our midnight guide to Zilom.

"Here's Kerevenn," I say to Jacob as the Ulux reaches the bottom of the staircase, moving slowly to take in the doors swinging open and closed as The Cendryll kicks into life, transporting its members above ground or to spectacular realms where wonder awaits.

"Slow travel," Yoran says as Kerevenn approaches, gaining a puzzled look from the three of us. "To Zilom ...

slow travel and subtle movements. In the land of suspended rain, people are more sensitive to storms."

With that, he offers his usual bow before spinning into the air, leaving Kerevenn to fill in the blanks.

"That made sense," Conrad comments, rubbing the back of his neck — a sign our journey to Rebel's Rest has taken its toll.

I know the perfect pick-me-up, placing my left hand on his lower back before moving it under his T-shirt: a gesture that brings a smile to his face.

"Easy, beautiful," he whispers. "I'm a tired mini legend."

"Size isn't everything," I tease as Kerevenn reaches us.

"Night Ranging appears to be keeping you busy," Kerevenn comments with a wise smile, choosing to stand on the edge of the busy Seating Station.

"She's just got in," Jacob adds, handing me the silver cup of Liqin. "Part of the rabble who hang out in Rebel's Rest."

I take his cup, finishing off his remedy designed to stabilise the mind. Liqin adds clarity to things, its sharp, bitter taste shifting any mental weight you're carrying. I'm not burdened by anything in particular, although I want to know more about Taeia's Night Ranger crew.

Any serious mistakes will mean an end to their time here, so they'll either wake up to the error of their ways or sink into insignificance. Taeia's never experienced battle which could be the reason for the chip on his shoulder. Either way, we'll find out what his problem is soon enough, including any lasting damage he's done, starting with a trip to Zilom.

"Farraday suggested we talk to you about Zilom, Kerevenn." I explain, standing on the bench of the Seating Station to level out the gap in height between us.

"Yes, he mentioned this in passing."

"Do you know what Taeia's lot have been up to?" Conrad asks.

Kerevenn nods, taking out a handkerchief to wipe away the residue that blights his vision. It's something he does a lot, the Ulux suffering from a genetic deficiency caused by a curse: giantism and rapid ageing the consequence of a curse they choose not to discuss. His grey suit matches the shirt and tie, white braces holding his trousers up.

Understated is the style of the Ulux but they're exceptional in more than stature: fierce wizards when fate calls them into action. Knowing this about Kerevenn makes me feel better about trusting him to guide us to Zilom. Not that I expect us to find trouble there since we're past bumping into evil wizards. *Rumblings* can resonate though, meaning we need to put a stop to whatever an unruly group of Night Rangers are up to.

"It sounds like Taeia's been ruffling a lot of feathers," Kerevenn explains as the doors on the ground floor swing open and closed, witches and wizards pouring in and out.

"He's taken it upon himself to add warnings and mild threats to Society figures who challenge his aggressive style," the ageing giant continues, "leading to a growing resentment of the young. You are the original young quartet, proving your loyalty on many occasions, but this could all be undone if the behaviour of a few becomes the norm."

"It won't," Conrad states in a defiant tone. "Too many people suffered to restore peace; we can't let one hot head undermine that."

"Indeed, Conrad," Kerevenn adds, "although another duel isn't the ideal outcome. Your intervention in Drandok was impressive, although your initial tone of suspicion could have led to a different outcome."

Conrad blushes at this, remembering our own touch of arrogance on arrival, staring down Orgev in a stand off that turned out to be misguided. It's a memory that makes me realise we've ruffled some feathers of our own, the principle of peacekeeping sometimes lost in the heat of the moment.

We haven't always adopted subtle movement ... the wise words offered by Yoran before he left us to our thoughts ... a sky urchin who's mastered the art of navigating troubled waters.

"The Domitus are a detached breed," Jacob adds in support of our initial suspicions surrounding the creature tamers. "When you add their unconventional methods, it's easy to draw certain conclusions."

"True, Jacob," Kerevenn replies, wiping his eyes again, "but the young amongst us run the danger of acting on false assumptions. This only feeds into the prejudice of those holding onto the belief that a certain age should have been upheld."

"Eighteen," Conrad mutters.

"Yes. Eighteen, Conrad: the age of official wizardry for centuries. You all helped to change this with your incredible bravery. Now is the time to hold on to the more innocent days when awe and appreciation dominated your actions."

"So, you think young Night Rangers are a bad idea?" I ask.

"Quite the contrary, Guppy. I think youth was the critical remedy missing for so long: the singular magical potion that ended up saving us all. *Humility* is the other essential essence of our world, however, always remembering how rare our magical landscape is; how fragile unity can be and, finally, how necessary it is to tread carefully in all circumstances. After all, it only takes a flame to start a fire."

With The Cendryll now full of Society folk, I ponder Kerevenn's words, holding onto the concept of caution. It's the theme of the morning — the concept of more considered steps — precisely what we'll need on our midnight trip to Zilom.

8

MERCURIAL MOVEMENTS

W e return to the Seating Station on the stroke of midnight, ready to head off to Zilom with Kerevenn who's dressed up for the occasion. Until now, I've never seen him in anything but grey: grey trousers, shirts and jackets, suggesting the memory of living in Sad Souls is etched into his mind. He's wearing a white suit with a dark blue shirt and tie: a picture of style and elegance.

The light's still muted in Sad Souls — land of the Ulux — although the sun peeks through now and again, bringing the reclusive giants out of their homes that stretch towards the sky. Kerevenn's made his home in The Cendryll now, about to guide us to a land of suspended rain: Zilom. I've flown over the place with Conrad before, but have never been drawn to what's on offer below.

Like all realms beyond The Society Sphere, there's no above-ground world to worry about, meaning magic is displayed proudly — in Zilom's case, the suspended rain that hangs in the air like an enormous chandelier.

Farraday's obviously suggested Kerevenn for a reason.

After all, he knows we can look after ourselves but our friendly Ulux has put us straight on the *decorum* needed on this trip. Yoran's words echo in my mind as the sound of the lift signals Kerevenn's arrival: *slow travel and subtle movements.*

I've got the feeling there's a certain way of navigating the suspended rain in Zilom, meaning our Williynx won't be needed tonight. The sound of the lift returns my thoughts to the job at hand, following Conrad into the lift as we greet our tall, stooping guide.

"An exercise in friendly travel," Kerevenn states with a smile, dabbing at his eyes with a handkerchief.

Conrad hands the ageing giant a vial of Crilliun: a nice gesture to illuminate his vision.

"Thank you for the offer, but a Ulux's curse is also a blessing. Darkness is no barrier to our vision."

"Cool," Conrad replies, administering the magical eye drops before handing me the vial.

"So, we're meeting your Night Ranger comrades by Merrymopes?" Kerevenn asks.

I nod, blinking as the Crilliun eyedrops improve my night vision. The Quij sleep at night, leaving only the moonlight to decorate The Cendryll's skylight. Conrad buttons his grey overcoat as the lift door shuts. A wall of buttons lines one side of the lift, Kerevenn pressing the letter 'M' as we rise, tapping his large feet on the S.P.M.A. logo carved into the floor of the lift.

The lift jolts halfway up, suddenly going sideways to transport us to the famous milkshake and ice cream parlour: a place offering Lucy and Noah some alone time.

"I take it you know little of Zilom," Kerevenn prompts as the lift jolts again, hovering in mid-air as a door appears in the darkness: our pathway to Merrymopes.

"We've flown over before," Conrad replies, opening the lift doors and uttering 'Entrinias', causing the door floating in the darkness to move towards us.

"Does the suspended rain work like Periums?" I ask.

"Yes, Guppy, although like certain realms beyond The Society Sphere, entry is not guaranteed."

"So, the illuminated strands of rain are a welcome signal?"

"Correct. The colour of the strand of rain must match your penchant stone. It's a sign your family is respected and welcomed by whoever activates the strand."

"So, they'll be able to see us once we arrive?"

"Of course, Conrad. We live in a world of magic, after all."

We jump through the floating door as it opens, leading us into a kaleidoscope of colour and the sweet wonders of Merrymopes ice cream and milkshake parlour.

"How annoyed are the Society elders?" I ask as the lift makes its slow descent, fading into the darkness.

"The majority tolerate Taeia's crew, recognising the arrogance of youth. Others are ready to teach them a lesson, which is where you come in."

"Me?"

"The four of you: Conrad, Lucy and Noah playing an equal part."

"Which is?" Conrad asks as we move along a hallway decorated by spinning colours.

The Merrymope twins who run the place are dramatic, meaning everything does something — from the spinning walls of colour to the leather booths that take you to The Revolving Room below.

"To represent the true essence of Night Rangers: mercurial service."

Kerevenn emphasises *service* to reinforce the point he made this morning — that we're guardians not guards; servants not superior sorcerers.

"And how do we prove this?" I prompt.

"By following my lead," Kerevenn replies as we make our way to the end of the dizzying hallway, leading to the sight of a spark of love ... Noah about to feed Lucy ice cream until they spot us.

Lucy's adapted her look for this evening, abandoning the jeans-and-baggy shirt look, choosing a skirt, T-shirt and black denim jacket. It's s subtle change but enough to take Noah's mind off the milkshakes. Conrad picks up on the romantic moment, sitting alongside Noah in the leather booth and closing his eyes, hoping to be fed the ice cream.

He gets a kick for his trouble but the moment's enough to solidify the beginnings of something — the smile touching Lucy's face suggesting milkshake wasn't the main thing on the menu this evening.

"So, ready to sing in the rain again, Conrad?" Noah teases, finishing off the ice cream.

"Who said anything about singing?"

"I just thought after your performance in The Singing Quarter the other day, we could have another bet on the way — see if you can hit every note."

"No bets tonight," Kerevenn states, using his forefinger to taste the *Belly Blitz* ice cream. "If any of you arrive singing, it will be viewed as another mark of disrespect. Zilom isn't The Singing Quarter or Rebel's Rest; it's a moving landscape of magic, much of it resting in the sky.

"The sky?" Lucy queries as Noah burps loudly.

"Yes, Lucy: the sky."

"And we *don't* need Williynx tonight?" I ask, glancing at

Kerevenn who seems more interested in the ice cream than our midnight trip.

"We'll take a different flight path tonight," our friendly Ulux replies. "Remember, this is a healing mission: no Quivvens, no weapons and no duels."

WITH ROMANCE IN THE AIR AND CRILLIUN ADMINISTERED, Kerevenn sits on the edge of the leather booth in Merrymopes, studying the floor as it vanishes beneath our feet, descending slowly to The Revolving Room where we'll dial ourselves in. There's always some form of fun on our evening travels, Conrad racing Noah to the dial in the centre, neither paying full regard to Kerevenn's request for no bets.

Noah wins this time, cheering as he slaps on the brass dial, only to find himself spinning in the sky as Conrad nudges him in frustration. A simple Magneia charm gets him back on his feet, jostling with Conrad as they both dial our location in.

I'm holding onto the iron pole in the centre as The Revolving Room teeters on its axis, spinning at a wicked speed until an image of falling light appears in one of the doorways. With no Williynx or Quivvens for protection, we accept Kerevenn's word about not needing protection: atonement the only mission tonight.

"We'll journey together," Kerevenn states as we press our bodies against the walls of The Revolving Room, easing closer to the vision of falling light. "Look out for a multicoloured strand of suspended rain, representing the combined colours of our penchant stones."

"So, don't touch any others?" Lucy checks.

"Correct. Many will be lit up — welcome gestures to the many others visiting Zilom."

"Sounds like a busy place," Noah comments.

"Zilom moves in waves, meaning we will be surrounded by Society comrades one second, then completely alone the next. Stay focused on the task at hand. Others may offer us welcome which we'll decline politely, explaining we're on Society business."

"Won't they take offence at that?" I query, ready to jump into the realm of falling light.

"Not if we decline with grace: a lesson your Night Ranger comrades would do well to learn."

"Taeia's not the sort of person that learns," Conrad adds. "He thinks he's arrived."

"Arrivals can be as brief as exits," Kerevenn states as we jump through the Perium as one, ready to address the rumblings in a magical realm that hovers in the sky.

9

ZILOM

The streets of Zilom are like a magical merry-go-round of light — the sight of people zigzagging in all directions, offering brief hellos as they brush their hand against their beacon of welcome: a fine strand of suspended rain lit up just for them.

The place is as pretty as I thought it would be, the spectacular vision of rain literally *hanging* from the skies, covering the streets masked by a thousand strands of light. It's like standing in the middle of the world's biggest chandelier, only this one's got moving parts that transport you on.

The air is warmer than expected for this time of night, adding a sense of comfort to proceedings. Kerevenn was right: we're not going to need Quivvens or weapons this evening. Adjusting the belt on my black leather trousers, I wait for a wise guide to lead the way as a group of youngish wizards appear to my right, moving carefully between the suspended rain towards their particular beacon of welcome.

I can't help thinking of the section of Zilom hovering in the sky, hoping the place we're headed to is up in the clouds.

"Remember, we're looking for a multi-coloured strand of light, including the combined colours of our penchant stones," Kerevenn states.

"But there're *loads* of them," Noah comments, swaying as a circle of suspended rain brushes against him.

"Nice dance," Conrad teases before the same happens to him.

"A strand is only activated with your hands," Kerevenn explains, smiling at the sight of Noah and Conrad swaying one way then the other, careful not to make contact with the strands of light.

"You could have said," Noah complains, putting his hands in his trouser pockets.

"Don't stop dancing now," I tease. "You were just finding your rhythm."

"There," Lucy adds, pointing to a multi-coloured strand of light off to our left.

As we turn, a flood of Society folk appear, dressed for a party by the looks of things. Maybe Zilom's party central, making this place more interesting by the minute.

As Kerevenn steps towards our illuminated strand of suspended rain, I catch a glimpse of the party crowd approaching their own beacon of welcome — a blast of music greeting them as they vanish through.

"I'm definitely coming back here," I whisper to Conrad as we follow our trusted guide. "A party in the sky!"

"Looks like we've got to win a few people over first," Conrad replies, pinching me as we walk, causing me to lose my footing.

I reach out with my hands to break my fall, almost brushing against a blue chandelier of light surrounding me — my fall halted by Kerevenn's call of 'Magneia'.

"Full attention if you want to make amends this evening," Kerevenn advises.

"Making amends for something we haven't even done," Noah challenges, retreating from his desire to complain as Kerevenn looks on.

"You are representatives of a new breed of Society soldier, Noah, marked by glory and duty. Your duty tonight is atonement for the actions of a misguided few: a duty which will fall on others in the future. Get ready for a different form of flight."

It's fair to say our guide for this evening's fun is a bit of a beacon himself, the pristine white suit glowing in the halo of falling light. Maybe Kerevenn's on a romantic quest of his own — the reason he offered to guide us here. I've got romance on my mind too, hoping I can sneak Conrad into my bedroom when we get back to The Cendryll.

For now, though, I need to stay focused on the job at hand: a meeting with frustrated comrades, questioning the role of young Night Rangers. With another posse of witches shimmering into view, giggling as they spin towards their entrance point, we place our right hands onto our floating Perium, careful to follow Kerevenn's instructions.

Right hand first, followed by the left, placed on the falling rain beam at exactly the same time ... then feet wrapped around it as it lifts us up, showering us with colour as it does.

"*Wicked*," Conrad comments as we lift off the ground.

It feels like we're on a fairground ride as our light beam begins to spin, sending our feet flying outwards as we rise higher.

"Yes!" Lucy shouts as we're spun faster, surrounded by a blaze of multi-coloured light.

I'm used to flying in the air but not so happy with the

spinning part of this mode of transport, hoping we get to our destination soon so I can gulp a large dose of Fillywiss: the remedy for dizziness.

I want to be clear headed when we meet the group who've taken a disliking to underage Night Rangers. I just hope we don't have to spend too long convincing them we're not like Taeia's crew, leaving us to explore the floating magic of Zilom for the rest of the night.

It's fair to say that sleep's becoming more of a pastime than a habit these days — the price you pay exploring in the day and ranging at night. We've all got different types of exploring to do, starting with the tail end of this journey which ends abruptly when Kerevenn tells us to jump off.

———

WE LAND ONTO INDIVIDUAL PATHWAYS OF LIGHT ... EACH ONE matching the colour of our penchants. Aside from the pathways, nothing else can be seen in the cool air so we follow Kerevenn's lead, continuing on our pathways until a frame forms around each of us.

"What are they?" I ask, pausing as the outline of a large hallway surrounds me.

"Signs of welcome," Kerevenn replies, ambling along as if he spends most of his time walking in the air.

"Why are we surrounded by different things?" Lucy queries — the skirt and rock-chick vest holding Noah's attention.

"Because we all have different hosts."

"So, we've got more than one group to win over," Conrad comments, staring up at what looks like an umbrella hovering over his head.

Noah's got a ladder and Lucy's twirling in the circle of

hoops floating around her: a brilliant sight of moving spaces in a realm I've never witnessed in all its glory. Flying over Zilom is *completely* different to arriving on foot. You get the light show from the sky but not the intricate detail within ... as if the morphing magic is only on offer to those who choose to immerse themselves in the place.

It seems we've still got a lot to learn from sky urchins and Ulux — two of the oldest species in the S.P.M.A. with knowledge as deep as their respective wounds. With the shimmering visions expanding around us, I ask the obvious question: "What now?"

"We each take our path to our awaiting host," Kerevenn replies, adjusting his blue tie before he reaches for the wisp of light above his head.

On contact, the strand of light explodes, sending Kerevenn *on* — the word he uses to explain magical travel. I've got no plans to hang around all night so wave to the others, adding "See you on the other side" as I move along the hallway stretching ahead of me: a glittering entrance that seems to go on forever.

I LOSE SIGHT OF CONRAD AND THE OTHERS MOMENTS LATER, turning back to see only the fading pathways of colour. Kerevenn better be right about this place, instructing us to abandon our Quivvens and Williynx for the journey.

It always feels better to see the glow under your skin: the sign of the Quivvens' protective energy. Penchants lose their power beyond The Society Sphere — one of the reasons Night Rangers travel with feathered creatures for company.

Travelling with a companion who can shape shift and blast ice is always reassuring — a walk along a *massive* hallway not so much. The longer I'm out here, walking in mid-air with nothing but a faint outline of light for company, the more likely I am to reach for my magical, morphing steel. Zilom's a *stunning* place but until I see proof of the welcoming spirit Kerevenn talks about, I need to be ready for all eventualities.

The midnight breeze lifts as I continue along the hallway, pausing when the surrounding outline fades away: time to reach for my Vaspyl. The last thing I want to do is reinforce the negative view of Night Rangers in Zilom, deciding to adopt Yoran's advice of subtlety over suspicion.

If anyone knows the art of negotiating alien territory, it's the wise sky urchin who appeared this morning in The Cendryll, offering help with Jacob's class and wise words for me.

"Gentle steps," I whisper, keeping the Vaspyl in my right hand, fighting the urge to transform the morphing steel into two swords: my weapon of choice.

The fact I can barely see ahead of me doesn't help either — my all-black attire giving me the appearance of a different type of sky urchin floating in the air. Patience is the essence of this game, I realise, sensing I'm being watched as the pathway rises up head, stretching into the darkness.

The Crilliun eye drops are working wonders, offering a degree of reassurance as I walk on, fighting the urge to activate defensive charms. It's part of a test ... to see if I'll react like Taeia's crew ... instinctively going on the offensive in a realm of comrades with spectacular imaginations. There's plenty of wonder in the S.P.M.A. although some realms take your breath away: Zilom clearly falls into this category.

I reach the sharp incline stretching into the midnight sky, feeling the cool breeze on my skin as I begin the ascent. Someone's waiting at the top ... a sudden sense I get as I climb towards a starless sky. It's strange to think I was taming Silverbacks a few days ago in Drandok.

Unlike Drandok, Zilom has a *weightless* energy as if it's never been touched by dark sorcery, making me wonder what's waiting for me at the end of this skywalk. The answer comes seconds later in the form of a strikingly thin figure standing on the edge of my pathway to the heavens. The figure only turns when I'm a few feet away, out of breath and desperate for the toilet, but I suppose that's going to have to wait.

"Greeting, Guppy Grayling," the mystery figure says, turning as he does, and I find myself staring at a man with the brightest eyes I've ever seen. He's got the gaunt features of a sky urchin with the elegance of a Society elder: an intense wizard I recognise but can't place.

"I know you," I state, not fully at ease in his company.

"Indeed you do," the mystery man replies, gesturing for me to join him on the edge of the skyway.

I decline politely, asking what he's studying from the precipice he balances on.

"You'll have to step towards the edge to see."

"See what?"

"The story of a Night Ranger destined for darkness."

This comment urges me on, keeping my distance from the imposing wizard as I reach the edge of our skywalk, looking down into a blizzard of light and action in the midnight sky.

"Taeia," I mutter as I reach the edge, watching my Night Ranger comrade hover on his white Williynx, firing out charms to clear the glittering streets of Zilom: a vision of a boy destined for darkness.

10

A WIZARD'S WISDOM

The image filling the chasm below shimmers with each movement I make, as if its stability comes from the people studying. I'm not afraid of heights but remain on guard, unable to place the hollow-cheeked, dark-skinned wizard standing alongside me.

He's close enough to make contact — a quick swipe of his hand sending me falling into the glimmering image of a Night Ranger crew causing chaos on the streets of Zilom. Part of me is wondering why I've been chosen to see this ... the archway of light calling me on ... leading me to consider who the others have met in this morphing realm of wonder.

Nothing's coincidental in the S.P.M.A. so whoever's agreed to meet us all has a particular role in this unfolding mystery. From the look of things, the mysterious, middle-aged wizard studying the image of chaos below has the focus of his resentment in his sights: Taeia's crew throwing their weight around in a place where the brilliant and bitter operate from the skies.

Taeia's no threat to any witch or wizard with the necessary skill and bravery, but he's clearly building a list of enemies that want to take him down. The second puzzle of the image I'm staring at is how it could have been formed here. It's clearly a past image of the streets of Zilom. The streets were peaceful when we arrived — the party crowd the most dramatic thing on the streets of suspended rain.

I'm still hoping to get to that party but my strange host hasn't said a word since I decided to take a leap of faith, standing on the edge of our skywalk.

"A Now-Then in a different form," the strange wizard states, explaining how a past image has been formed.

A Now-Then is shaped like a spinning top, having the ability to recall past events when you spin it in the place the event occurred. *How* my intense host has got a Now-Then to touch the bottom of the cavern is something I'm sure he'll get to, preferring to focus on a vision of the past that might shape our future.

I watch as Taeia laughs, whipping out a swirl of light towards the scattering Society members — members who spin out of sight as their palms reach their suspended beacon of welcome.

"How does it work? The Now-Then, I mean?"

"Williynx feathers," the elegant wizard replies, removing the feather decorating the lapel of his suit. "A Now-Then is limited by the location of the event; Williynx are only bound by their magical potential which is vast."

"So, *any* Williynx feather can generate a past image?"

A shake of the head follows this comment. "Only the feather of a Williynx present at the event."

"Taeia's Williynx," I reply, watching as my host flicks the white feather into the air.

It floats horizontally, spinning out a tapestry of light until another image is formed ... of our little duel with Odin and Neve Blin in Drandok.

"It seems an error has been made in placing power in the hands of the young."

"We were attacked by Odin and Neve. We tamed the Silverback and saved Odin from a brutal death at the same time. Also, as we're on the subject of errors, secrecy turned out to be a *big* error for us — something every Society member agrees on — and something the young amongst us risked their lives to put right."

"Spoken like a true Fire Witch, lacking doubt or fear."

"Fear isn't my thing. Also, I don't mean to be rude, but I thought I was here to help put things right. Taeia's arrogant and in love with himself, but I had no idea he was up to this. No one's mentioned it in the Cendryll or anywhere else on our travels. If he *is* up to something though — something more than stupid boy's games — I'll happily help to bring him to justice."

"Which is where we're aligned, Guppy, as I hoped we would be. We've both seen war and have the Society's best interests at heart. Our meeting tonight will help to ease resentments in Zilom and beyond. Taeia's crew are the exception and not the norm, as I've argued on your behalf, but it still needed a meeting to confirm this belief.

Recent engagements in various realms have caused a semblance of suspicion, and we both know where doubt can lead. Meeting your Night Ranger crew face-to-face was a necessary act to remove all doubts. Now, the focus turns to a young man with bitter blood. The simplest solution would be to strip Taeia's crew of their status, but The Orium Circle sense something darker in him: the Renn who will live to see glory."

"Glory?"

"Yes ... glory in the skies."

I glance at the skill sky from our high vantage point,

wondering what glory lies in waiting for a Night Ranger with limited magical gifts. An heir to power with bitter blood sounds like another collision course in the making.

"So, Taeia's going to be a problem."

"In time, yes. Charming enough to draw allies towards him and *insecure* enough to seek dominance over others."

"So, why not just strip him of his Night Ranger status?"

"It's deeper than that, Guppy. It's not simply a case of rounding him up and housing him in The Velynx. He's under eighteen so too young for imprisonment. Neither can we rehabilitate him for the same reasons."

"Meaning?"

"Meaning you need to join forces with them. A temporary measure to gauge Taeia's energy, distinguishing between *the fun* he argues he's having and the *intention* behind his acts. It needs to be done quickly, giving the three comrades he rides with a chance to prove their actions are based in high spirits, as opposed to high handedness.

Taeia's path is set, but the others still have a chance at redemption. Many things have been put into place to sustain a lasting peace, and the Society elders only use expulsion as a last resort. Also, a psychopath above ground is as much trouble as one in our midst."

"And you've got the authority to arrange this?" I ask. "No offence meant, but doesn't this sort of move need to be agreed by The Orium Circle?"

"It has been."

"You must be a fairly important wizard."

"Just a soldier doing his duty, trying to keep a low profile to allow my nephew to forge his own path."

"Who's your nephew?"

"One of your Night Ranger comrades."

"Noah?"

He nods. "Noah doesn't want to live in the shadow of a famous uncle, and he isn't on the best of terms with his father. Each of your friends is currently meeting someone senior in the Society: a wise guide leading them to the source of unease.

"Who are they meeting?"

"Figures who will become more important in time."

"And where do I know you from?"

"Varakel ... on the trail of a colossal beast."

That helps me to make the connection, recalling the wizard who moved in a blizzard of speed, dodging the roaring army of Silverbacks blasting into the caves. He moved silently, never pausing to confirm battle strategy, but his gifts were obvious: precise in dress and movements.

"Aarav Khan," he adds, finally offering his name. He then utters 'Undilum' to deactivate the shimmering vision below. Brushing a hand over his suit, he turns his attention to the second image floating behind us, allowing me to step away from the edge.

"I promised to give Noah space, 'not raining on his parade' as the above-ground world like to put it. Therefore, I will clarify matters of concern and be on my way. Your duel in Drandok proved two things: the collective skill of your Night Ranger crew and the intuitive ability you are legendary for.

It would have been easy to exercise unnecessary force when you tracked Odin and Neve down but, instead, you remembered the compassion offered to you by another Society legend."

"Casper Renn," I say, thinking how alike Kaira's dad and Aarav Khan are: intense, elegant and majestic in their use of magic. It's fair to say I'm pleased he's on *my* side, feeling bad

for Taeia's crew when they come face-to-face with him —
which they will.

"Well, at least it's good to know we're not throwing kids
in The Velynx."

"Cruelty is an outcome of extensive corrosion when a
magician's spirit is beyond repair. Your mother's chance at
rehabilitation is an exception to this rule."

"I suppose people are bitter about that."

"Naturally, but the comrades who saved her from a
worse fate had legend on their side, allowing them to nego-
tiate a passage of rehabilitation for your mother."

I recall everything Casper and Philomeena Renn did for
me and my brother. After all, they're the reason my mum
isn't in The Velynx, and why I'm still alive to tell the tale.
Deep down, I know I want to be like them when I'm older:
regal and fierce at the same time — my reputation enough
to make malevs freeze. Wouldn't that be cool?

"How do things work here?" I ask, moving onto the
strange architecture of Zilom all of which is formed of light.

"Everything in Zilom is imagined in real time: the path
we are standing on, the images we've been studying and the
many worlds suspended in the sky."

"*Worlds ...?*"

Aarav Khan offers, the bald head and intense eyes less
unsettling now. He's got a mystical look about him, seeming
to float on the illuminated pathway we stand on.

"The Society for the Preservation of Magical Artefacts is
truly infinite in scale. Held together by our most precious
artefact — The Devenant — the map of magical wonder
continues to stretch with our imaginative powers. It is a delicate balance between beauty and unity, and one I would
encourage exploring when your Night Ranger days are
behind you."

"Can we explore a bit of it now ...?"

"Of course, when your friends arrive."

I ponder this, looking at an unclear image the white Williynx feather has created: a star of light offering a view onto silhouettes of buildings and people I can't make out.

"So, apart from the suspended rain that takes you to your destination, the rest of Zilom hovers in the sky?"

"Yes."

"*All* formed temporarily from creative charms?"

"The Bildin charm, to be precise."

"And things just vanish when people get bored?"

"Why the surprise, Guppy?"

"Well, it doesn't sound very *stable*."

Aarav laughs for the first time, making him seem more human which puts me more at ease. I'm used to intense wizards but he's on a whole other level: the dark skin, hollow cheeks and bald head adding to his mystical energy.

"You only need stability with gravity," he adds, and with that the glittering pathway disappears, leaving us hanging in the air moments before Conrad, Lucy and Noah come into view: the signal for my mysterious host to vanish.

"Nice place to hang out," Noah adds in one of his weaker attempts at comedy, glancing at the disappearing vision of his uncle without saying a word.

I'm hoping this isn't another family drama we're going to have to skirt around as Kerevenn appears alongside me moments later, returning my attention to the hidden wonders of Zilom. Offering me a powder-blue Williynx feather, he says:

"A feather from a friend."

The feather from my favourite Williynx — Laieya — who's been free to explore her chosen realms of the S.P.M.A., clearly more limitless than even I'd realised. It must have something to do with gaining access to the sky realms here — the sight of the others studying their feathers reinforcing this.

"If you kindly follow an old giant," Kerevenn adds, releasing his orange feather into the midnight light surrounding us. He nods for us to copy him, completing the circle of multi-coloured feathers that form into liquid light.

"Now," Kerevenn explains, 'Entrinius' to request entry or 'Bildin' to build a world in the sky."

"I thought you were leading us," Conrad adds, glancing at the turquoise light dripping from his hand and hanging in the air.

"I have my own meeting to attend to," Kerevenn replies with a smile, adjusting the lapel on his white suit: another signal he's on a date.

"Well, don't stay out too late," I say before turning to the others and asking, "Where to?"

Lucy studies the yellow light falling in raindrops from her hand. "Let's decide before we build something we regret," she replies.

"Like what?" Conrad asks.

"I don't know: a firework or a raging beast, maybe."

"I thought I was your raging beast?" Noah jokes, rediscovering his comic timing as we get ready to explore. "Come on, let's see where the party's at," he adds before uttering 'Entrinius', transforming his fire-red liquid into a balloon.

I smile at the idea of stumbling across a party in the sky, morphing my handful of light into a party hat. Our adult guides have left us to explore: a friendly giant hoping for a party of his own, and an uncle deciding not to cast a shadow over his nephew's night.

11

ALONE TIME

We don't find the party, realising the 'Entrinius' charm isn't enough to gain access to private dwellings. Zilom isn't like anywhere else I've visited in the S.P.M.A., meaning we have to forge our own world with the handful of light in our hands.

It's been a busy night so we decide to take our own path: two couples ready to find a romantic spot in the midnight sky. It's less about *finding* than creating so I throw my handful of light into the air, pivoting as I spin it into a glittering circle. As the circle hovers in the air, Conrad joins in, using his handful of tanzanite light to add stars within the circle.

We laugh as we add to our romantic vision, catching the glittering raindrops that fall towards us, shaping them into a swing: a simple vision for some well needed alone time. I look back to see Noah and Lucy decorating the Zilom sky with their own romantic touches: a more traditional pathway that stretches upwards.

They walk along it hand in hand, Noah finally waking up to the fact that love isn't blind adoration. Zoe Tallis was a mirage whereas Lucy could be the real thing. As Conrad and I swing towards our circle of stars, I offer a wave to them, catching Lucy's smile as Noah places a hand around her waist — the two of them ready to find their own private space in a weightless sky.

Part of me wonders how you access the hidden places of Zilom, laughing as Conrad and I swing closer to the circle. Maybe it's the raindrops of light that are falling around us, something to do with catching enough of them in your hand and uttering an unknown incantation. As much as I'd love to know, that doesn't matter tonight because my focus is on the boy next to me, planting a kiss on his neck as we swing into the circle of stars.

We're pulled through the first band of light until another one appears ... the vision I've just whispered into life ... circle upon circle appearing as the old ones fades away, allowing us to stay suspended in the Zilom sky for as long as we like: a perfect stage for a girl who needs a break.

TIME HANGS IN ZILOM LIKE THE SUSPENDED RAIN ... SILENT and comforting as if nothing else matters but the moment you're in. It's weird how things feel different here, helping you to forget everything for a while.

It's certainly helping me to forget what's around the corner: an agreement to ride with Taeia's crew on our next evening of Night Ranging, hiding the fact we're joining forces to check out the group who are ruffling so many feathers.

Conrad and I talk about this now, asking each other about the mysterious people we met on our different walkways forming as Kerevenn waved us on: a gentle giant on his own romantic mission.

"So, what did you make of Noah's uncle?" Conrad asks, holding my hand as we swing slowly in the evening sky.

"Intense."

"Noah didn't say much when he saw him."

"Aarav said he likes to give Noah space — that Noah's not keen to live in his shadow."

"Fair enough."

"So, how's Seyena? Still as humourless as ever?"

Seyena Follygrin is a sky rider legend from Gilweean. I made the mistake of gawping at her tiny size when I first met her, leading to me being dragged towards her with a Magneia charm. It's fair to say she put me in my place, making the distinction between size and *power*.

She's powerful all right — one of the people who helped Conrad to master the art of sky riding. She's the figure who appeared at the end of Conrad's walkway tonight, resenting Taeia's Night Ranger antics as much as anyone else. Seyena isn't someone you want to get on the wrong side of.

"You need to get over your little mishap with Seyena," Conrad adds, holding out his hand to catch a raindrop of light.

"She didn't need to *drag* me to her."

"You didn't need to stare at her."

"Well, she's *tiny*."

"And you were rude."

"I bet you stared when you first met her."

"I kept my eyes closed," he jokes, rubbing the scar on his neck: a sign he's getting tired.

"So, what did Seyena have to say?"

"That we need to get closer to Taeia ... isolate him from the others to find out what he's really about."

"Checking on his bad energy?"

"Exactly."

"Sounds like he's destined for dark deeds."

"That's what Aarav senses. Let's hope he's wrong."

"I mean, Taeia's weird but is he *really* on the way to becoming a dark wizard?" Conrad queries.

"Time will tell although he's bound to sense we're up to something."

"Doesn't matter," Conrad says, putting an arm around my waist. "He's out of luck either way."

"I wonder how Lucy and Noah are getting on," I say as we swing a little higher.

"I'm sure they're doing just fine."

"It's a shame we can't stay here all night."

"Who says we can't?"

"You look tired."

"We haven't had much sleep lately."

"You've got a way of keeping me awake."

"I can't help my irresistible charm," Conrad adds, running his hands through his copper-blonde hair.

I enjoy the feeling of being close to him again. Night Ranging can make time fly, putting more importance on time with loved ones. It's also important to hold on to the magic: a thought that makes me study the silent space around us.

"What do you think would happen if we jumped off?" I ask, edging closer to Conrad.

"We'd use the raindrops of light to break our fall, probably," Conrad replies, the look on his face suggesting he isn't up for another free fall.

"Or we could swing closer to the circle of stars and jump through; it's bound to be a Perium back to The Cendryll."

"You're relentless, Guppy Grayling."

"I thought you liked my relentlessness," I tease.

He pulls me closer, looking for a different type of adventure. "I say we swing as high as we can, working out how we access other places hiding in the sky."

"Deal," I add, laughing as we kick our legs to generate greater velocity, reaching out with my left hand to catch as many raindrops of light as I can.

"Maybe we'll find a castle in the sky," Conrad says with a smile, reaching out to gather his own handful of suspended rain. "Come on, let's see what else Zilom's got to offer."

We swing our legs harder, laughing as we light up the night with new visions, hoping to gain entrance to the secrets of the silent skies.

Our sky dance leads us back to Lucy and Noah who we find sitting on top of a bridge. It looks like The Sinking Bridge in The Singing Quarter: an interesting statement from a couple who were only friends a few days ago.

The bridge stretches across the Zilom sky: a perfect panorama to rest on. Conrad and I weren't lucky enough to stumble across other private spaces as we swung higher, leaping through our circle of stars, deciding to build a ladder of light that took us higher until the bridge came into view. Maybe Zilom is exactly what Kerevenn said it was, each strand of suspended rain representing a beacon of light, only on offer to welcome witches and wizards.

As Night Rangers drawing suspicion in the S.P.M.A., it makes sense that people aren't keen to offer entrance to their hidden spaces, so we're back with our friends, sitting on the edge of the bridge as we discuss our mysterious hosts

— each one reinforcing a different aspect of the plan to fly with Taeia's crew on future evening missions.

"So, we all need to get close to someone in particular," Lucy explains, adding how the person waiting at the end of her path was Weyen Lyell: scarred legend of The Orium Circle. Weyen and Seyena's appearance means the rumblings are spreading, so we'll have to move quickly to quell rising fires. "I've got Fillian."

"What?" Noah replies with obvious jealousy.

"He's a moron who follows Taeia's every step, so don't waste your energy on him," Lucy replies, adjusting her skirt.

"He's also a creep, particularly with girls."

"Don't worry, handsome" Lucy adds with a touch of her old sarcasm, "I'll use a Fixilia charm on his privates to keep him in check."

The puzzled look on Noah's face makes me laugh, wondering who I've been assigned to.

"Taeia," Noah replies, adding the wise guide waiting for him didn't give a name, only that we needed to act quickly.

"Did you recognise him?" Conrad asks.

Noah shakes his head, adding, "They were dressed in a grey tunic that sort of hung off them. Oh, and they didn't have any eyebrows."

"That's it?"

"Yep. A big tunic and a tiny head."

"How old was he?"

"*She* ... about thirty."

"Did she have any hair?" I ask, not quite knowing why.

"*Massive* hair," Noah adds, making me wonder if he's making all this up. "It sort of went *on and on.*"

"Like you are," Conrad jokes, feigning a yawn.

"Are we keeping you up?" Noah adds, used to the friendly jostling with Conrad.

"I'm missing my beauty sleep."

"I could make you a pillow for your pretty head. I mean, if I can make a bridge ..."

"Okay, lover boys," I say, sensing we'll need to leave soon. "You can get back to your arm wrestling soon. Let's stay focused on the mission ahead."

"Did she say who you and Conrad need to keep an eye on?" I prompt, assuming the woman actually spoke to Noah

"I've got Mae and Conrad's got Alice. She wasn't the talking type; she wrote in the sky."

"Before she evaporated in a raindrop?" Lucy adds, looking a little tired herself.

"No, it was more like this," Noah replies, tilting forwards before he *falls* off the bridge, tumbling into the darkness.

"*Noah!*" we all shout, jumping off together.

There's no Williynx to swoop us up and Noah isn't activating the flight charm, so something else is needed. Luckily, he doesn't leave us in suspense for too long, holding his arms outright to control the tumbling motion.

As he falls through the air in an upright position, he reaches out for the nearest strands of suspended rain, pulling on them as he falls. The beacons of light stretch into diagonal lines, drawing other strands towards Noah until he's got a parachute of light to guide his fall.

"Grab on!" he shouts towards us as we tumble through the sky.

I fly past Noah, struggling to grasp the suspended rain as I fall. It's a *lot* easier than it looks, like trying to grab onto water. Conrad appears above me, yelling in frustration each time another handful of raindrops slip through his hand. It's as if the suspended rain is only designed to take you *upwards*, suggesting the silent lady with the missing eyebrows drew more than names in the sky.

"Stop snatching at them," Noah says as he manoeuvres his parachute closer to us. "Let the first few slip through your grip, getting a sense of your energy, then *pull*."

"Maybe you could have shared that information *on the bridge*," Conrad shouts, trying to kick out at his friend.

"Stop whining, sky rider, and do what you do best: find the rhythm of flight."

That's enough to get Conrad over his tantrum, closing his eyes as he descends through the midnight air, letting his hands run along the nearest rain beams illuminating the sky. He's in his element ... a boy born to be a sky rider ... feeling for the moment to pull the magical chords into action.

I choose my own rhythm, keeping Lucy in my vision who successfully pulls the two beacons of light, forming a parachute from the surrounding suspended rainfall. It ends up being a matter of *touch* ... something Noah obviously wanted to show rather than explain. It's a *brilliant feeling* once I know I'm not about to crash to my death — floating through a magical, midnight sky towards who knows where.

In a weird way, it doesn't really matter because I'm happy to hover in this new world of wonder: a realm where time seems to stand still and anything can be created from the suspended rain: pathways, romantic visions and parachutes. There's *nothing* like the S.P.M.A. so I hold on to our final moments in Zilom, planning to return as soon as we've dealt with the Night Ranger who's making waves.

12

THE CHATTERING TAP

The Chattering Tap is unusually busy for such an early hour — Conrad and I deciding to end our morning flight early to head to The Winter Quarter and the reliable mind of Joseph Flint. Although he's had a little slip up recently, notably with Alice Aradel, Joseph's a gentle soul who natters away to himself in his usual position at the bar.

The seven-strong army of the Tallis family serve the regulars — sociable comrades basking in the peace and beauty of The Winter Quarter in the early hours. We sit at our favourite table by the window, looking out at the perpetual snow decorating the streets.

Above ground people can't see this section of The Winter Quarter, only getting soft light and eccentric shops for their entertainment. Eccentricity is the very thing we're relying on this morning, hoping Joseph Flint's brilliant mind can weave its way through our recent journey to Zilom.

We went there to make amends, meeting powerful hosts on the way — some familiar and some not. I'm reminded of

Aarav Khan's words, regarding the dark path Taeia's on. Trust has been fractured by a single group of young Society soldiers, meaning *all* Night Rangers are under the spotlight.

Aarav said as much, suggesting a distinction between intention and impulse needed to be made. I didn't get the feeling he doubted my loyalty; he knows my history but history doesn't guarantee loyalty, meaning mine's going to be tested again.

I'm up for the test, particularly when it involves protecting the Society I love. Joseph will give us the low down on what Taeia's been up to, already looking nervous when he catches sight of us sitting at our favourite table near the window.

He's dressed in his familiar ripped robe, muttering to himself as Lorena Lenant slams his glass of Liqin on the counter. He pays in Kyals — Society money — before taking a big gulp, maybe guessing the reason for our visit. Rebel's Rest is our main hangout, rowdier than The Chattering Tap with less chance of being thrown out if you blow something up by mistake.

Sometimes magic and remedies don't mix, particularly when you decide trying out a few untested charms is a good idea. Everything's fixable, of course, the Repellia charm returns all things to their former glory as long as they're not marked with curses.

It looks like Taeia's on a cursed path — not that I think he's using dark magic yet. He's always had a need to prove himself — a Renn with *very limited* magical abilities. He got into the S.P.M.A. by the skin of his teeth, struggling to make friends while he gathers enemies of the wrong kind: Society legends watching his every move.

Conrad and I have the morning to ourselves, leaving Lucy and Noah to catch up on romantic developments; we'll meet up at midday, preparing to join up with Taeia's crew. It's really a monitoring mission although it definitely won't have been sold in that way.

We don't get on with Taeia's lot but will have to put ill feeling aside. Society duty comes first and testing loyalty is the order of the day. Fillian Crake, Mae Tallis, Alice Troper: the trio of sheep that hang off Taeia Renn's every word.

Let's hope they haven't followed his every move, otherwise the Telynin remedy will be used to extract every piece of information, followed by another touch of magic, making them forget they ever stepped foot inside the S.P.M.A.

I fought hard for peace, carrying scars on my legs and arms as uncomfortable medals, so it's a little sad to think that my own comrades are the ones stirring up trouble. Trouble only itches these days — not like before when it raged until the fires almost got out of control — but it's trouble either way so we'll be back in the skies soon.

As Lorena Lenant makes her way over to us, I leave Conrad to order the drinks, smiling at the sight of comrades appearing in portals of light on the winter streets, about to embark on another day of magical living.

JOSEPH FLINT JOINS US AT THE TABLE AFTER HIS THIRD GLASS of Liqin is slammed on the bar alongside him — a nod from Lorena Lenant in our direction, signalling this remedy's on us. For a wizard with a taste for Jysyn Juice, he's certainly getting through the remedy for delusion and hysteria, mainly caused by the mind-bending Mantzils haunting Quibbs Causeway.

Since our little catch up in The Shallows, Joseph's been a bit wary of us, doing his best to control the nervous tremor in his right hand. When he gets *really* nervous, he loses control of his glass, sending it flying through the air. The last one smashed into the wall, soaking Lorena Lenant — probably the reason for the excessive force she uses every time she slams the glass down next to him.

Joseph's all smiles as he sits opposite us, placing his satchel on his lap as he lifts his robe off the floor. He's weirdly protective of his satchel and robe — two things that have seen better days — although I wonder if it's more *us* than him: our presence, I mean. The last time we bumped into him, we got into a little fire fight with Alice Aradel.

Ever since, Joseph sends a nervous glance our way, never staying long once we've arrived. I start to get a bit edgy myself, watching as his tremor gets worse. I'm not keen to be soaked with Liqin so decide to put him at ease.

"Morning, Joseph. We've got a favour to ask."

"A favour ...?" he replies, frowning as he glances at Conrad.

I nudge Conrad, gesturing for him to ease up on the intense stare.

"Yes, Joseph, a favour and we couldn't think of a better mind to ask."

"Well ... I ... I like to pride myself on my extensive Society knowledge."

"Better than anyone else's," Conrad adds, offering our eccentric friend a smile.

"And what might this favour be?"

"Information," I reply, studying Joseph's reaction as I sip my hot remedy.

"Regarding?"

"Some recent shenanigans."

Our nervous comrade frowns again.

"Some kids throwing their weight around," Conrad explains, adding, "Not us."

"I wasn't suggesting anything of the sort ..."

"I know you weren't, Joseph, but it's better to get it out of the way."

"Do you have names ...?"

"Taeia Renn," I reply, sensing the recognition in his expression.

Joseph holds on tighter to his satchel before he speaks, glancing out at the snow-covered streets as if he's expecting company. "A crew of wayward minds."

"How so?"

"Due to their travel and arrival. *Blunt instruments* unable to apply the skill and subtlety required of Night Ranging."

"For example?" Conrad asks, leaning in to catch Joseph's whispered words.

"A desire to be *more,* particularly the boy burdened by the name 'Renn' ... flaunting his Night Ranger status to anyone who questions him ... casting suspicious light where no suspicion lies."

"You've seen this?" I question, following our eccentric comrade's gaze as it turns to the white sky — soft, silent snow touching the window outside.

"Yes, Miss Grayling. Many have, particularly the more vulnerable who are easily moved by the weight of authority."

"What have you seen?"

"Clearing streets where there's no need, using harmless charms in unnecessary ways. Entering peaceful establishments to question people at random, sighting 'rumour' as their justification. Drawing more volatile members into minor battles for sheer pleasure. Nothing *sinister*, you see, but all leaving a sour taste."

"And they stick to their given route each evening?" Conrad asks.

"No, Master Grayling. They *roam*, seeking adventure in untroubled realms. The concern is obvious ... that our wayward comrades will eventually draw sleeping soldiers to their door ... Society legends able to quell naïve notions of power with a flick of the wrist."

"But they must know," I add. "The legends you talk about: The Orium Circle, Casper Renn."

"Indeed they do, but this sort of intervention will only happen if the alternative fails."

"Us," I say, remembering Aarav explaining the plan to join forces.

"Yes. A Shadow Strike, Miss Grayling: similar to the intervention used with me recently."

"You were just trying to help a fallen comrade," Conrad adds. "Unfortunately, she had a habit of doing harm so we had to track her down. We're pleased you didn't get into trouble for it."

"Which I'm indebted to you for, Master Grayling. Returning to the question of our lost boy, it has raised questions regarding the age of entry once more."

"Meaning we're screwed if things get out of hand," I add, remembering the looks of resentment I got in my early days: the first under age member to be allowed entrance. That all changed with Kaira's arrival, forcing a change to established rules that might be reversed if Taeia doesn't get a grip.

"Your sacrifices guarantee your place in our magical world," Joseph adds, steadying the tremor in his right hand by placing it on the table. "It would, however, be beneficial to future generations of young witches and wizards if this issue could be resolved quickly.

Scribberals are busy day and night, airing the grievances

of many. Your kindness and loyalty will shine through once more — as they did when tasked with my 'troubles'. If they had not, I may not be sitting with you now."

"We had good teachers, focusing on mercy as much as magic," I say, offering Joseph a smile. "Hopefully, we can find a way to pull Jacob back from the path he's heading down."

Humility is the invisible magic of the S.P.M.A., Farraday once told me, the critical component required to balance power and duty. If we're not careful, we'll have younger members roaming above ground, firing off charms for the hell of it until the strange sightings can't be explained away. The thought of wayward young wizards makes me think of Jacob.

I'm beginning to understand the reason he looks so tired all the time; it's not just the manic nature of the students but the responsibility of training them in this balancing act of power and duty. It only takes *one* slip to start tongues wagging above ground. I've got no intention of returning to a world without magic so I finish off my drink, adjusting the belt on my black, leather trousers as I stand.

"You're a legend, Joseph," I add, deciding to shake his hand for some reason. "And sorry for having to turn up the other day. It was Alice Aradel we were after, and you brought us right to her."

"It's a shame it had to end this way for Alice," Joseph replies, scanning the crowds on the snow-covered streets, "but I accept she chose the wrong path." His tremor hides a fear he might have said too much, but if Taeia's crew think they're going to start hassling vulnerable wizards, they've got another thing coming.

It'll soon be time to call Laieya and Erivan from their resting place in the skies, transporting us to a new task of managing wayward magic. It's still early, though, meaning Joseph can go back to talking to himself at the bar and I can watch the snow outside with Conrad.

"I bet Taeia's looking forward to seeing us," I joke, nudging Conrad as he sips his drink.

He always smells good and looks even better — a thought that seems to be running through Lorena Lenant's mind: the barmaid with a hollow smile. Thankfully, Conrad prefers substance, tracing a finger over the faint scars on my wrists.

We share a wild story ... of a time when the Society rocked on its heels, creaking as darkness gathered and swarmed. Now, we track questionable comrades wherever they're hiding, preparing for whatever drama Taeia Renn's got in store. He hasn't got the firepower to compete with us, meaning he'll either retreat or lose his cool.

"I feel another song coming on," Conrad says, rubbing my wrists to keep me from dwelling on the task at hand.

"You hate singing," I reply, sipping my warm remedy — Srynx Serum this time — helping to heal wounds. I've got no new scars but the old ones have traces of curses, meaning they've never fully healed. The orange remedy soothes the itching when it gets too bad.

"It must be the snow that's inspiring you," I say to Conrad, surprised he hasn't got other things on his mind. We've got the rest of the morning to ourselves, leaving time for some 'personal adventures'.

"You're all the inspiration I need," he jokes, clearing his throat as if he's about to blast out a tune.

"You should stick to Jysyn Juice."

"It doesn't get me in the mood," he replies, offering a mischievous smile.

"So, you've got the song to get *me* in the mood?"

"Yep."

"Which is ...?"

"You'll have to wait and see. Drink up."

"Why?"

"Because you've got to dance along, obviously."

"What's Lorena put in your cup, love potion?"

"No need to get jealous. I can't help how handsome I am," he jokes, running a hand through his hair as if he's on camera.

This draws the laugh he's been hoping for as I study his tanned face and arms, wondering if we should find somewhere warm, leaving the Bing Crosby moment for another day. Conrad's got that mischievous look in his eyes, though, so I go along for the hell of it. We're surrounded by snow and fizzing portals of light, so why not add a song and a dance to the mix?

Squeezing his waist, I whisper, "Come on then, Casanova before I change my mind."

I take one last sip of the Srynx Serum, enjoying the warm glow it gives me, laughing as Conrad spins me around when we stand from the table. Joseph Flint offers a wave as we leave The Chattering Tap: a comrade who seems more at ease now he's part of the solution rather than the problem.

13

UNFINISHED BUSINESS

Pat's Caff sits in darkness on the quiet, evening streets of Founders' Quad although there's a buzz of activity in the secret space where Night Rangers gather. Steel pods hang in mid-air, held up by a myriad of magical charms, making the gathering remind me of a group of astronauts about to take off on an important mission.

Our midnight mission carries a bit more weight tonight because it's the first one where we'll join forces with Taeia's crew — the rebels who are rubbing people up the wrong way. I get the feeling they like to make people uncomfortable, meaning tonight should have a bit more spice than normal.

Taeia claps at the sight of us arriving, offering his usual sarcasm and bitter smile to our evening get together. Noah calls a vacant steel pod towards us, whispering something to Lucy as Conrad stays close to me, sensing my rising anger.

If it was up to me, I'd work on getting a rise out of Taeia, exposing his hollow credentials to the busy room, but that would only reinforce the idea that young Night Rangers are too volatile to trust. Instead, I bide my time, knowing it won't be long before his anger gets the better of him.

I'd rather be in Merrymopes, to be honest, tucking into a Belly Blitz and watching the night go by. Instead, I've got to keep company with a Renn who doesn't deserve the name. It's weird how Taeia doesn't remind me of Kaira at all. The Renns carry their power lightly, probably because their magical history is so rich.

They have more legends in the family than many others put together, but then most families also have a runt in the litter and I'm staring at one now: a handsome hot head about to become a has been. The one thing all Renns share is good looks and Taeia's no exception: the flawless, mixed-race skin and lithe figure making him look more like a model than a sleeping soldier, but that's where the good news ends.

There might be beauty on the outside but it's definitely lacking within. He's arrogant and domineering, sneering at people he doesn't like or respect. I get the feeling I'm on his naughty list, judging from the laugh he shares with his underlings. I wonder if he'll be laughing when we take him down, which is precisely the plan once we find out what he's getting up to at night.

I've been paired up with Taeia, ready to drench his ambition whatever that turns out to be. Aarav Khan senses dark energy within him which is hard to argue with. I mean, if a mystic's getting bad vibes, that *can't* be good news.

"Ignore him," Conrad says as we climb into our steel pod, placing our penchants on the edge to direct it upwards, towards the space next to the comrades forced upon us.

All the other Night Ranger crews are friendly and enjoy the fun the job brings, realising how lucky they are to have been chosen for the role: all of them except Taeia's lot who act like the warrior way is their destiny. The only problem is, they've never been near a war let alone fought in one, something I like to remind them of when they get above themselves.

"I'll ignore him until he pushes too far," I reply, keeping my gaze fixed on the athletic lot who are sprawled out in their steel pod. They always have to be above everyone else, manoeuvring their pod as close to the ceiling as possible for a hollow sense of superiority. Pathetic, I know.

"The Fire Witch to the rescue!" Taeia shouts out as we get level with him.

It's the line he always uses when I have to suffer his company, obviously his way of trying to make me feel uncomfortable, but I can also sense his weakness in the faltering smile and need for reassurance.

"The one-trick pony strikes again," I counter, returning the insincere smile.

I can tell Conrad thinks I'm going to do something stupid, but I'm not risking my place in the S.P.M.A. for a halfwit like Taeia Renn He'll get his comeuppance soon enough. The others — Fillian Crake, Mae Tallis, Alice Troper — follow his every move, their feet hanging over the steel pod. I laugh at the sight of them, knowing this will move us onto the conversation of joining forces.

"What's so funny, Grayling?" Taeia asks, telling Fillian to shut up: a lanky, athletic type who sulks like a six-year-old.

"You."

"Getting cocky before we head out for the night? You must be on the lookout for surprises."

"You're the most unsurprising person I've ever met."

"You need to keep your girl in check, Conrad."

"You need to watch your mouth," Conrad replies, "or we can start the night with a little friendly fire."

"Brave although we can't use magic against comrades so, as always, you're all bluff."

That's his first mistake, grabbing onto the steel pod as Conrad utters 'Disineris' to shatter the base, sending Taeia's crew hurtling towards the floor.

Conrad's already out of our pod, floating down towards them courtesy of a flight charm.

"*Move*," Noah orders, urging Lucy and me to follow Conrad as the crew we're teaming up with extricate themselves from the web created to break their fall — a look of rage on their faces.

"If he gets me kicked out, I'm going to kick him in the balls," Lucy whispers as we land on the ground. The other steel pods hang a little lower in the air, the Night Rangers occupying them looking forward to a bit of drama.

"Keep Alice company," I say to Lucy, adding, "Noah can deal with Fillian and I'll spin Mae into submission. As long as we keep Taeia's back up occupied, he won't dare make a move."

"And if he does?" Noah queries, readying his defences.

"He'll be begging for mercy in no time."

I catch a glimpse of our Night Ranger audience hanging over the edge of their pods, betting kicking in as bags of Kyals are retrieved from Keepeasies.

"You want a fire fight," Taeia hisses, spinning the arc of blazing light around his hand, "then let's play with fire."

Conrad stands opposite him, arms by his side with no defensive charms activated: a clear sign of the contempt he has for the hollow soldiers we've been forced to partner with. We've got the scars of war and Taeia's trading on a name: a name that won't help him if this gets out of hand.

"Losing your nerve," Mae says to me with a smile I'm about to wipe off her face.

She doesn't see the Ozzer in my hand, realising I don't need anything more than a balancing device to keep her in check. I throw the Ozzer above her head, watching as she sways back and forth, unable to get her balance.

Now it's a stand-off between Conrad and Taeia, Noah and Fillian and Lucy and Alice: two Night Ranger groups facing off against each other as the slow clapping starts inside Pat's Caff. The clapping's a reminder we're all tasked with a job tonight, meaning our little ruckus needs to resolved; it's a clapping sound Noah decides to copy close to Fillian's face.

Noah's gesture camouflages the Zombul in his hand, releasing a sound that causes Fillian to scream, scrambling for the exit as the mind-splitting screech of the Mantzils flood the room — our suspended audience ducking for cover.

Noah's performance is over seconds later, the sight of him standing perfectly still dressed in his usual outfit of chinos, T-shirt and waistcoat not quite fitting with a wizard who's filled the space with a taste of venom. He had no intention of releasing the mind-blistering creatures found on Quibbs Causeway, something that would *definitely* get him into trouble.

It's a simple statement of superior moves and counter-moves, and enough to put Taeia and Alice in their place ... the pair grimacing as the Mantzils' screech fades along with the fury marking Conrad's face. The shadow strike will come in time — no trip to The Velynx needed.

We're kids, after all, allowed entry by the very people who can pull the rug away, so I return to the idea of gentle movements: a phrase I'm beginning to like more and more. We're not dealing with Domitus or taming dangerous creatures, our reactions needing to reflect the challenge facing us.

We're on a search and rescue mission of sorts, uncovering the cause of the massive chip on Taeia's shoulder before it cracks into an endless chasm. I don't know if he's got darkness in him or not, but I'd prefer a non-fatal duel than a death dance with a boy who's worst crime is delusion.

"Let us know if you want to take the night off," I say in a parting gesture, deciding I should add the element Taeia seemed so keen to use: fire.

Uttering 'Smekelin', I blow the ball of fire upwards, stretching it out into a carpet beneath the steel pods above us. The occupants make a hasty retreat, realising I'm going to fill the place with fire ... more to drive the point home than destroy ... that if you trouble waters for long enough, you'll end up with a storm.Conrad, Noah and Lucy add the necessary water, dousing the flow of fire as Taeia's crew crouch in submission.

"Ozzers and Zombuls are party tricks," Conrad says, glaring at the soaked crew who are too disoriented from the Mantzils' screeches to activate a Velinis charm — no bubble of light protecting them from the flood of water arcing down. "If you *really* want to fall out, just say the word and we'll give you some scars to remember us by."

Standing in our multi-coloured bubble of light, helping to keep us dry, I glance at Fillian, Alice and Mae sensing they've been taken off course by a boy with something to prove. They crouch meekly, eyes closed as the water splashes down over them, looking genuinely stunned at what's just happened.

Taeia's a different story, refusing to lower his head as the fire's extinguished by the water, not wanting this to be his first submission. Something about him reminds me of my mum: the detached manner, maybe, or the thirst for power.

Three adults pivotal in my life saw this in my mum and pre-empted a complete collapse, choosing sensitivity over abandonment. Mum's a Melackin, yes, but at least she isn't trapped inside The Velynx. I hope we can find a way to do the same for Taeia, not really knowing why I feel this way, except for the fact that I was given a second chance after mum's betrayal, so maybe it's my turn to be the redeemer.

"See you in The Shallows," I say as we fire a Promesiun charm through our bubble of light, directing it towards the ceiling where it rests. The ceiling lights up like a lighthouse beacon: a signal for our Williynx to lift us back into the night sky.

14

SKY RIDERS

We meet our feathered companions in The Winter Quarter, standing on The Sinking Bridge before we head into the skies — ready to meet up with the questionable crew who've just had a taste of our friendly fire. It won't stay friendly for much longer if they're up to no good.

They're like a group of peacocks, needing to display their powers as a means of marking out their territory. It's more insecurity than anything else for most of them, although this doesn't change things. Tonight's about tracking their movements, picking up on habits that led to a meeting in Zilom.

Aarav Kahn senses bad things from Taeia Renn, and it's our job to put this theory to the test. What better place than The Shallows to start our surveillance: a peaceful place in a floating quarry where magicians come to rest.

Alice Aradel made the mistake of appearing there, thinking she could drag Joseph Flint into her dark world. Luckily for us Joseph's movements were being tracked, leading us to the evening witch who's now tucked up in The Velynx.

It's a *big deal* being a Renn in the S.P.M.A. They're probably the most famous family in the Society although, unlike Taeia, they carry their magical legacy with ease. This is probably because each member of the Renn clan is gifted with rare magical abilities — except for Taeia, that is.

He goes against the grain in every way, from his arrogance to his magical failings. He's about as far away from a typical Renn as you can get, so I'm already formulating a plan to get him back on track. Conrad, Noah and Lucy are going to hate my idea, meaning I'm going to need all my persuasive powers to get them on side.

For me, the bottom line is it's better to have a Renn on your side than against you, and the last thing we need is Taeia discovering his magical powers in the wrong company. Keeping Joseph Flint out of Alice Aradel's clutches was pretty easy in the end, mainly because of the evening witch's reputation and the fact that Joseph wouldn't hurt a fly.

There's no shifty witch or wizard influencing Taeia's movements as far as we know, so we need to get to the bottom of this before he's kicked out of the S.P.M.A. for good.

"They're a bunch of weirdos," Noah comments as we stand on The Sinking Bridge.

He'll return here soon with Lucy on their first formal date, placing their penchants on the bridge to see if they can light up the water below: the symbol of love.

"Taeia needs a slap," Conrad adds, making me realise my plan to redeem a lost boy is going to need a lot of work.

Why I'm still pursuing this plan is still a bit of a mystery, but if I've learnt anything from Casper and Philomeena

Renn, it's the importance of compassion — which isn't the same as ignoring potential danger.

If the crew we're about to fly to The Shallows with *do* have darkness buried in them, it will be exposed soon enough, but three of them are sheep which leaves one lone wolf: a mixed-race boy lacking all the qualities of his namesakes.

We should at least look for the cause before applying the consequence. I mean, if we'd jumped to conclusions two years ago, Isiah Renn would have been locked up in The Velynx with my mum.

Until they've *actually* done something bad, they'll stay in the 'questionable' category, although it looks like Conrad and Noah have already made their minds up.

"Now we've got to babysit them," Conrad comments, adjusting the penchant ring on his forefinger.

"Let's just see how it goes," Lucy suggests, standing alongside Noah who's looking unusually agitated. "We've already proven we can control their tantrums, so I doubt they're going to be much trouble."

"It's the trouble they're causing that's the issue," Noah adds, running a hand through his mop of black hair. "Trouble that's making us look bad."

"Taeia's at the root of it," I add. "The others are just following on."

"*Obviously*," Noah replies with a roll of the eyes which annoys me.

"I mean we need to study Taeia ... work out what the root of his problem is otherwise we'll end up just like them, throwing our weight around every time we're challenged."

"We'd never do that."

"We just did," Lucy replies. "Guppy's right. We can't go around arresting everyone that makes a mistake. The main role of Night Rangers is to keep the peace, using subtle interventions where necessary."

"So, we make friends and pretend nothing's happened?" Conrad queries, turning up the collar on his grey coat.

"No, we just take it easy and do what we do best: *assess* before we strike. Whatever they're doing can't be that dangerous or they would have already been kicked out."

"Meaning?"

"Meaning Farraday arranged the trip to Zilom for a reason. He chose us specifically, probably because we've made our fair share of mistakes."

"So, we're being tested as much as Taeia's crew are?" Lucy prompts, following my point.

"Maybe ... to see if we can show the same compassion we were offered. Let's face it, I was a bit of a whirlwind when I arrived, running into an Ameedis attack in the first few weeks. We're hardly dealing with something like that, are we? So, maybe it is a test, keeping us in check as much as those we're tracking."

"Reigning in our friendly fire, you mean?" Conrad adds, the intense look softening.

I nod, putting an arm around his waist. "I think so. The danger of magic is getting lost in its power."

"Guru Grayling," Noah jokes as he buttons his waistcoat. "I like it. I'm feeling calmer already. Hungry, actually."

"You're *always* hungry," Lucy adds, laughing with a new glint in her eyes.

"It's all this talking; it's making me woozy."

"Too many big words?" I tease, getting a splash of water in my face for my trouble.

Two can play that game, I decide, responding with the same water charm Noah's activated. I'm not one for splashes, deciding a deluge is probably more fun, the three of us bursting into laughter as the blast of water drenches Noah.

I'm astride Laieya in seconds, tapping my feet to activate my Williynx into action — a vision of blue lifting off from The Sinking Bridge before Noah can react. Conrad and Lucy spin into the sky with me, leaving us to call down to Noah who's ignoring the soft squawks of his fire-red companion.

Things get more comical when Noah stands on the bridge, head hung as he dips into a fall. He's the dramatic one of the quartet, grabbing every opportunity to perform. This performance starts the race to the portal in the sky ... Noah's Williynx swooping below as he's about to hit the water, spreading its wings to lift him towards us.

He's got me in his sights, hoping to get his own back but I'm already ahead of the pack, Conrad chasing me as I close in on the swirling band of light in the sky, ready to transport us on.

"You're going down, Grayling!" Noah shouts, shaking his arm in comic fury.

"You need a towel!" I shout back as Laieya surges upwards, shape-shifting into a smaller form as Conrad and Lucy close in on me.

At least it's lifted the mood before we return to more serious business: a Renn who could be falling from grace.

TAEIA'S CREW ARE WAITING FOR US ABOVE THE FLOATING carpets of white weeds in The Shallows, his white Williynx signalling their position. They're hovering in a line high up in the evening sky, sitting proudly astride their feathered friends who don't look as keen to be transporting them. No

Williynx allows a dishonourable member to climb aboard so, for now at least, the suspect group are tolerated by the majestic creatures from Gilweean.

If I'm right about the miserable four, Mae, Alice and Fillian are weaker characters. They're probably just happy to have been made Night Rangers, possibly falling under the illusion that a Renn leads by nature — the reason they don't seem to question anything they're told. The next few hours will reveal more, starting with activity in Poridian Parlour and how our arrival is treated.

We don't go there much although when we do things are fine. I'm always conscious of my age, knowing the scars I've earned aren't badges to be flaunted. There are thousands of soldiers with better stories than mine so I try to tread carefully, hoping some subtle magic will avoid another duel: magic of the *human* kind. Time to get inside the head of the boy on the white Williynx, without Conrad trying to rip his head off, that is.

He's not going to like what I've got in mind, but tonight's not about us; it's about trying to save a lost boy from a fall. We were both lost once, stranded in a Society of adults without parents to protect us, forever thankful that two adults took us under their wing, so it's time to return the favour — or at least try.

"They don't look very happy to see us," Lucy says as we glide towards them, the evening wind lifting my long, brown hair.

"Well, we did almost drown them," Noah replies, patting his Williynx reassuringly.

"Let's take it easy," I suggest. "Adapt to their rhythm."

"And what if they play up again?" Conrad asks.

"We'll do what's necessary."

"Well, here's to joining forces with nutters," Lucy adds as

we near the sullen four, surrounded by a feint fire charm to dry out their clothes.

"So, what now?" Taeia asks, keeping his gaze lowered for the first time.

"We follow your lead," I reply, picking up on his subdued energy.

If anything, he's more depressed than dangerous although dark moods can take people to *strange* places.

"Let's go," he says without further explanation, shooting ahead on his white Williynx towards the floating buildings lighting up The Shallows: our first stop on a night of eventful travel.

EVENTFUL TRAVEL

P oridian Parlour has the usual evening bustle — all four rooms full of Society members debating, interacting or taking a break from all things magical. My Night Ranger crew follows Taeia's, watching his every move as his mood darkens: an arrogant boy already put in his place.

I'm going back and forth about my view of the lost boy blessed with the name Renn, wondering if the others are right and I'm wrong. What if he *is* dangerous and the rest of the whole group are unhinged? Are we going to have another duel or simply mute their magic before kicking them out for good?

What will Taeia be like above ground if that happens? He won't have any memory of the S.P.M.A. but I doubt his character will change much, meaning we might have a problem either way. I still think it's better to try to tame him, quelling his frustrated fire before it gets out of hand.

The only problem is Conrad isn't going along with this theory, still seething after Taeia's 'your girl' comment. Also, I've never seen Noah so annoyed, the humour we all love him for parked temporarily — his hands in his pockets, ready to release whatever magical trick he's got planned.

If the mood doesn't change soon, we're in for another light show in Poridian Parlour, only this time our comrades are likely to fire back with full force, leading to one of us going down. I know who my money's on. We get the expected looks from the witches and wizards filling the games room, the noise of multiple competitions of Rucklz filling the room.

Elin Farraday glances over, nodding towards me with a knowing glance. I imagine his brother's told him all about our trip to Zilom, including what it might mean for the future of Night Rangers. I love my role in the Society, flying through the skies or whizzing through Periums, and I'm not about to give it up easily — so it's time to study the mixed race boy struggling with the burden of a famous name.

Taeia walks over to the corner of the games room, sitting at the vacant table that only has four chairs. If he's trying to make a point about who's in control, he's failing. His authority's fading fast and he knows it, staring at the floor as loud cheers fill the room, Elin Farraday winning another game of Rucklz.

Farraday is a family name although the one I'm closest to uses this as his first name — the Farraday in The Cendryll that is who put us on our current path. I've never found out his first name and he's obviously not keen to give it up. It's probably embarrassing but he's a legend so no one really cares. Anyone willing to carry a lethal artefact during an all-out war doesn't need to explain himself, and Farraday fits into this category.

Part of me wishes he was here now, whispering one liners to us as we start our mission of discovery. With our Williynx perched on the window sill in much smaller forms, looking like a line of colourful ornaments, I study the crowd of adult wizards sharing whispered thoughts to one another.

Hopefully, they all know why we've suddenly appeared with the suspicious lot causing problems. If they don't, they soon will because no one's talking ... that's until Conrad gets bored.

"So, what's the plan?" he asks, stepping closer to Taeia who lifts his head.

"We sit here for a while."

"What for?"

"To work out what *this* is."

"You know what it is. You've been throwing your weight around and we're here to find out why."

"Why don't you just ask?"

"Why would we trust what you say?" Lucy challenges, unbuttoning her black denim jacket.

She's kept up the more feminine style of dress I've encouraged, abandoning the boyish look that wasn't doing anything for her. Noah's definitely noticed, staying close to Lucy whenever we travel together.

"Who made you the boss all of a sudden?" Fillian queries, rotating his neck as if he's limbering up for a fight.

He's obviously forgotten our little rumble in Pat's Caff already.

"Have you got a problem with a girl asking you questions?" Lucy challenges, standing her ground as Fillian rises from the chair, towering over her.

"I've got a problem with being blamed for something I haven't done."

"That's funny," I say, stepping alongside Lucy as I blow on my hands, making our lanky comrade know I'm *always* ready to end an argument, "because I was looking at a vision of the four of you last night?"

"And where would that be?" Mae asks as a sarcastic smile forms.

She's a blunt object with more testosterone than most boys, reminding me of a mini weight lifter. The physical power doesn't extend to her brain though, making it easier to get her to pipe down.

"In Zilom with Aarav Khan."

That shuts her up and makes Fillian sit back in his chair. To be honest, I was a little unnerved by Aarav initially, keeping my distance from his intense, dark energy until he showed me the vision of the very Night Ranger crew sitting at the table now ... Taeia guiding his lot to fire down charms over the witches and witches scattering for cover. It was a game, obviously, but not the sort you'd get away with for long in a place like this.

"What, you mean our fireworks in the sky?" Alice adds with a bitter laugh. "It was a bit of fun, for God's sake. Are you telling us you don't have fun when you're out at night?"

"You think it's fun to fire at your comrades?" Conrad prompts as a worrying look crosses his face.

"Not *at* them," Taeia challenges. "*Around* them. No one gets hurt so what's the problem?"

"The problem is the resentment you're building up," I reply.

"With who?"

"Look around, lost boy. Look at the faces staring over at us. Do you really want an army of legends hunting you down?"

"Adults would never harm kids," Fillian comments.

"Which is why we're here," Noah counters, grabbing a glass of Jysyn Juice off a passing tray.

"Sounds like a threat, Khan," Taeia replies as his mood

darkens, flicking something in his hands which I'm ready to counter.

The aim is to avoid another light show here, putting the Society elders at ease, but if it has to be done so be it. I blow on my fingers as the verbal to-and-fro continues, beginning to sense that I'm wrong about Taeia, the realisation dawning on me that he *is* on a dark path just as Aarav Khan suggested: a Renn beyond redemption.

"We don't need to make threats, Taeia," Noah replies, keeping his hands in his pockets to signal how at ease he is around this lot. "You should have worked that out in Pat's Caff earlier. After all, you're the ones sitting in soaking clothes."

"I hope we're all getting along," comes a familiar voice from behind us: Elin Farraday dressed in a purple robe with a large pendant over his belly.

"Trying to get to the bottom of things without any drama," I reply, offering Elin a friendly smile.

He could take out Taeia's crew with one move but our errant crew are right — adults would never attack an under age wizard so I check my impulsive nature, pushing back against the thought to whistle my Williynx into action.

Moving tensions to the sky might help with our assessment. After all, if what they're saying is true and their antics are only a game, we can have a game of our own on The Hallowed Lawn: a high-speed Rucklz tournament to test their reflexes and true intentions.

Jacob won't like this at all but he doesn't need to find out: a simple game to put the question of intentions to rest so we can squeeze some fun out of the night. I'm not a fan of uneventful travel, always wanting to add some spice to our evenings whether that's tracing danger or laughing till it hurts in Rebel's Rest.

"Let's hope that remains the case," Elin replies in what sounds like a friendly warning. "Disputes can be resolved in many ways and as this is a minor one, the solution should reflect this."

"Like a game of Rucklz, for example," I offer, sensing my opportunity.

"You want to sort this out over a board game?" Mae Tallis challenges with a sarcastic laugh, adding, "that's why they call you The Fire Witch."

She gets the expected laugh from the rest of her drenched comrades, the fire charm framing their bodies not doing much to dry them out. I've got a plan for that as well.

"Not a board game, Mae. An all action competition to find out what you mean by 'friendly fire'"

"You're on," Taeia says straight away, ignoring the worried looks from Alice and Fillian who seem to know something we don't. "Where?"

"The Hallowed Lawn."

"Deal, but don't go squealing to your brother if you lose."

The smile I offer Taeia makes him pause — a look he hasn't seen before as I rub my fingers together. He's got no idea what he's just signed up for: a dance with a girl who can tame Silverbacks and track down fallen Domitus to their hideouts.

"As long as things don't get out of hand," Elin Farraday comments, rotating the large pendant hanging over his belly. "Intense competition is all we are authorising. Anyone inflicting injury will face serious consequences."

"Understood," Conrad says as we whistle to our Willi-ynx, ready to blast through the stained glass window and into the evening sky, heading towards a sacred lawn where the mighty rest: a perfect stage to bring a lost boy back from the abyss or send him hurtling into it.

———

Spintz charms light up The Hallowed Lawn and Williynx feathers mark the boundaries. All things can be repaired in the S.P.M.A., meaning the Repellia charm will be used at the end of the tournament, returning every blade of grass to its original place.

Generally, this sacred piece of land is only authorised as a training ground, although I know Casper Renn will accept my reason for coming here. Essentially, I want to show Taeia his hidden potential, highlighting how *any* witch or wizard can improve their craft.

He might not be the most gifted Renn, but that doesn't mean he can't be a talented wizard. The Rucklz tournament gives me the platform to prove this point although I need the other's approval or things could go haywire. Noah's more on board than Conrad and Lucy but I stand my ground, reinforcing the point that we're about peace and unity. We need to at least try to remove the black cloud hanging over Taeia.

He's obviously got a sense of inadequacy evident in every comment and move he makes, desperate to prove his superiority. Only insecure people feel the need to do this so as I hover over The Hallowed Lawn, illuminated by a multi-coloured shower of Spintz charms, I go over my strategy with the others again.

"It's not about letting them win," I explain. "It's about guiding them in the ways of Night Ranging."

"Which they don't already know?" Conrad challenges,

patting his turquoise Williynx as we hover on our end of the pitch.

I glance down at the glittering dots decorating the The Hallowed Lawn, already knowing my starting point to kick things off, but I need everyone on board or the strategy won't work.

"Of course they know, Conrad, but they've veered off course for whatever reason ... just like my mum did, and your dad."

He pauses at this comment, struggling with a wave of grief that rushes through him. I hate bringing up his dad unnecessarily but my point remains — my mum and his dad were saved by the compassion of others so we'd be hypocrites if we didn't try to do the same.

"Okay," he mumbles, taking a deep breath as he removes his grey coat and tying it around his waist, "but only until they prove they don't want to be helped. Deal?"

I nod along with Noah and Lucy, adding, "Deal."

"What's our first move?" Lucy asks, getting a mischievous smile from me.

"Fire, of course," I reply, and the games begin.

A SHOT AT REDEMPTION

With the two teams in position, we wait for the Williynx to release their call to action, a loud squawk from each feathered friend kicking off the game. We've agreed on our battle strategy, starting with strands of fire to ease us into the game.

First, we need to activate one of the dots decorating the Rucklz pitch, swooping down to tap the sacred ground before we release our friendly fire. Things have to stay friendly otherwise we could be the ones in trouble.

We'd have to do something really stupid to get kicked out of the S.P.M.A., and since none of us have expulsion in mind we glide above the ground, surrounding ourselves with circles of fire. Taeia joins forces with Mae, leaving Alice and Fillian to take up the left-hand side of the pitch.

Their first strike is fairly obvious ... a diagonal attack with the Promesiun charm ... a faint strike to avoid wounding. Rucklz, after all, is a game of skill and wit and not something normally turned into a battleground. It's going to be up to our questionable comrades to decide if they want a fight or not: a duel they're not likely to win.

As the whipping light of the Promesiun charm heads towards us, we enact our first counter move, disappearing out of sight on our Williynx, re-appearing higher in the sky. It's one of the most complicated tricks to pull off, using a Disira charm on the back of a Williynx, mainly because it's not their usual mode of travel.

"That's not in the rules!" Fillian shouts up at us, firing out his Promesiun charm in frustration, but all it does is light a path towards him, Lucy spinning out of range as she counters with a Vaspyl ... morphing steel flying towards Fillian and Alice in the form of a spinning disc.

The object is easily shattered by Alice which is the point, trying to improve their reaction time and imaginative attacks: the art of wizardry, after all. They're too self-centred to accept guidance though, still under the illusion that their Night Ranger status offers them protection.

Everyone in the Society can enact magic, creating waterfalls and balls of fire or ladders to the heavens with the Bildin charm. Magic is no big deal in the S.P.M.A. although what you do with it is, so I decide to push a little harder, flying down towards Taeia and Mae to see what they've got in store for me.

Their second act is more surprising, working together to spin out of sight before appearing behind me in the air, using a flight charm to cast a web of steel in my direction, but I'm gone before it can make contact, directing the web towards Fillian who blasts it into a thousand pieces.

Conrad offers a genuine clap of encouragement to us all, adding "Good game," as he does so. He's always supportive even when he's not sure of my methods, spinning on Erivan to avoid Mae's arc of ice flying towards him.

Conrad reacts by tapping the neck of his turquoise companion, whispering for Erivan to release a cloud of mist to blind Mae temporarily, allowing him to use the Fixilia charm to tie her to the spot, seconds before she can activate a bubble of protective light. One down and three to go, Mae grunting in frustration as every move causes pain.

She's got a possible way out but it requires one of her crew to put themselves in the firing line. None of them seem to be keen to do this until Taeia vanishes out of sight, deactivating the flight charm to wrap the bubble of light needed around Mae.

The problem with this move is I've dismounted from my Williynx, hiding behind the protective curtain of a Verum Veras charm … inches away from where Taeia and Mae stand.

They're not likely to stay within the bubble of light so I track their movements, making sure I stay out of sight in the glittering blanket of light invisible to the naked eye. The plan's working so far, no-one stepping over the mark with any crazy explosions of charms, but I need to keep pushing on — the only way of finding out if there's hidden venom in their 'friendly fire'.

Mae steps out the bubble of light first, replacing it with a Weveris charm that wraps itself around her body. She reminds me of an Egyptian mummy as she pivots away from Lucy's fire birds, trying to bite their way through her protective blanket.

Mae's skilled enough to obliterate the birds with ice, but as she focuses on this she forgets about the missing piece: me. With a soft whisper, I blow on my hands to release a flurry of Quij into the tournament … bottle blue and orange insects buzzing with a rare intensity … just enough to form a mild blizzard around Mae.

The Quij are delicate, beautiful creatures who can carry a hundred times their weight. They're also a weapon if needed, turning into fire bullets on command. I'm obviously not going to *burn* Mae to death but I can distract her long enough to weaken the web around her, exposing her to the ice cage Noah's got ready.

She turns a second too late, whipping out a flood of water in an attempt to knock me off my feet, but I'm gone before it reaches me ... back on Laieya who's waited patiently in my glittering curtain of protection ... expanding into a *massive* form to stop the opposition in their tracks.

Laieya's now twice the size of her feathered friends, squawking as she joins Noah in the sky — her nostrils releasing an ice mist to signify a trap in the making.

"*Now*," Conrad orders and we release what looks like swords of ice towards Mae.

She panics, trying to spin a Disira charm into action but Conrad distracts Fillian for long enough to activate another Fixilia charm, keeping Mae frozen in position. Unable to move, she lets out a scream of fear.

It doesn't take much to freeze a foe, particularly those who've never experienced battle. It's all about rhythm really, something I learnt from Farraday in my early days of training. All Society soldiers are trained to the same level, but not everyone adapts their mind to similar challenges.

Rhythm is everything for that reason, knowing when to hover and when to strike ... when to dance and when to disappear and, critically, when to feint which is what we're doing now.

With Mae's screams filling the evening air, making me wonder if any Society elders are watching via Follygrins and Panorilums, I smile at the sight of the swords forming into a cage, whizzing round Mae to trap her and take her out of the game.

The game is going to plan, taking the opposition out

with minimal force until we're satisfied with the results. So far so good as all we get from Mae is some swearing and pointing in Alice's direction, as if it's her fault she lost sight of the enemy.

"Ready to quit," Conrad teases with a smile, happy my plan is playing out as I expected.

The last thing any of us want is to see a comrade expelled so we continue with our evening fun. We combine the Spintz charms illuminating the game into a roof of multi-coloured light, adding a stadium effect to The Hallowed Lawn which makes everyone smile — except for Mae, that is. *Boy* that girl can sulk, sitting out on the boundary offering no guidance to the others.

She should be acting as their eyes, pointing out our positions but instead she proves one thing about her errant crew: there's no unity between them. They're out for themselves — the thing that brings you down in battle.

"Let's take things into the sky," Lucy suggests as we reform for a moment, giving the opposition time to regroup.

"Above our roof of light, you mean?" Noah checks, getting a nod from Lucy.

"But that takes us outside the basic rules," Noah challenges, "having to activate dots to form weapons."

"We just lift the dots into the sky," Conrad suggests with a smile, offering a new formation of the game we haven't played before.

"Brilliant idea," I say, always happy to bend the rules when necessary.

"Happy to take things into the sky?" Conrad calls over to Taeia's crew. "Lift the pitch above the roof of light?"

We get a shrug from Taeia who replies, "Convinced we're not trying to burn the Society down now?"

"Not yet," I reply, "but it's going in that direction."

"Good, because I want to head back to The Winter Quarter and have some fun."

"Firing out at more comrades, you mean," Noah adds, unable to help himself.

"No, *sir*," Fillian replies sarcastically. "To have a drink and a laugh, if that's okay with you."

"Be my guest," Noah adds. "After we've won, that is."

"Then let's take it to the sky," Alice replies — and to the sky we go.

———

THE BOUNDARIES OF THE GAME ARE LESS CLEAR ONCE WE'RE hovering above our roof of light, the dots glimmering in the multi-coloured carpet we're now using as a pitch. It's a brilliant twist to Rucklz, meaning we can dart through the roof of light, continuing the friendly battle in two spaces — below and above our makeshift stadium.

Fillian's taken out of the game next, making the mistake of firing out two shields of steel, easily frozen by a counter blast of ice. Their reaction time is letting them down, something I point out when he perches beside Mae.

"You need to imagine multiple moves *before* you defend," I explain. "It's all about creative timing."

"We don't need your help to finish a game, Grayling."

"Well, you obviously do, Taeia, otherwise you wouldn't lose every time we had a fall out. I'm trying to help not rub it in so, maybe *listen* for once in your life."

"Okay. Teach me something," he adds with a strange look touching his eyes, as if I've triggered something in him.

Something tells me it's not appreciation.

"Okay, let's change the game and practice reaction time."

"Fair enough. You in, Alice?"

With a nod from his lanky comrade, Taeia crosses his arms astride his white Williynx. "What are we missing then?"

"The split-second timing you need to avoid capture. Rucklz is a game but real battle is a different thing all together."

"Meaning what?"

"Meaning you need to refine your intuition and counter moves," Conrad explains.

With the two teams hovering above the carpet of light, Lucy and Noah join in to give an example of what I mean.

"You get lost too quickly in your emotions," Lucy adds, "meaning you're not clear when you have to defend. We're on the *same side*, remember, whether we like each other or not."

"And you think we don't know that?" Alice challenges, tying her blonde hair up in preparation for a lesson she clearly doesn't want.

"If you knew it, you wouldn't think firing at your comrades was a game," Noah adds. "Guppy's idea of Rucklz is as far as games go between comrades. We know the rules and we agree to friendly fire. No one gets hurt and we spend time refining our skills: the perfect solution in a time of peace."

"Then teach us something before I fall asleep," Taeia adds, his feet swinging on his white Williynx.

"Okay," I say. "Move closer to us and keep a few feet apart. Conrad and Lucy will whip out a simple Promesiun charm but don't react in anger. Instead, imagine *every* way you can defend against it, including every way the Promesiun can be formed: circles, storms of light, webs, bullets etc."

"Yeah, I get it."

"And decide on one before you defend against it. You're getting caught in two minds, giving us the seconds we need to trap you. Let's hope we're never in a war again, but if we are you won't have those seconds to spare."

"Get on with it then, Grayling before we call it a night. I know my uncle helped to train you although he's refused to do the same with *me*."

"Why's that then?" Noah prompts.

"You tell me, Sherlock. Maybe he had enough of teaching kids after they ended up with scars. Not the legend he thinks he is, after all."

"Only one of the greatest wizards in the history of Society," I add, sensing my anger rising. "Something you're never going to be if you don't shut up and listen."

"Can we just *get on with it*?" Mae shouts from the sidelines below, still sitting on The Hallowed Lawn alongside Fillian. "You're little talk's getting a bit tedious. Put up or shut up, Grayling."

"As you asked so kindly, Mae," I reply with a sarcastic smile before returning my attention to Taeia and Alice. "Picture all possible defences and get ready. We'll only stop when you run out of ideas."

"You'll stop when you've won or lost," Taeia adds with a trace of venom. "That's the name of the game, after all."

"Fair enough," I reply, nodding to the others who prepare their charms — the moment the lost boy's mask slips and he fires out a blast of light towards me ... streaks of purple energy screaming through the sky ... energy that isn't pure in design.

The moment he releases his venom, Taeia's Williynx screeches in fury, whipping one way then the other as it struggles to free itself from him. He punches the side of his Williynx, causing a blast of ice to fire from every other feathered companion present, ripping Taeia off the majestic creature no longer on his side.

"Make sure he doesn't escape!" Conrad shouts as Mae, Alice and Fillian look on in horror.

Their stunned silence says it all: the realisation their self-proclaimed leader has succumbed to the darkness hidden within. As he falls, thrown off his white companion, Taeia spins to direct his fire towards two of his own crew ... causing me to free fall from Laieya ... firing out a wall of ice which thuds into The Hallowed Lawn around Mae and Fillian.

Frozen in shock, they cower as the purple streaks of venom shatter parts of the protective layer of ice ... an attack from a lost boy at the mercy of a Williynx army seeking retribution close in ... a boy forever staining the name Renn grabbing his chance to vanish out of sight.

QUESTIONS & RETRIBUTION

With Taeia abandoning his shot at redemption, I sit with the small gathering in The Cendryll, the skylight washing the ground floor with a soft glow. The adults sitting with us are familiar faces, spending their days overseeing day-to-day business in the faculty for charms.

Casper Renn and his sister Philomeena stand on the periphery of The Seating Station, firing out questions to assess the damage done.

"So, it was Guppy's idea to challenge Taeia's crew to a game of Rucklz?" Casper asks, unbuttoning his waistcoat.

Immaculate as ever, he glances at his sister who shares his elegance, her faint scars hidden by the suit dress and neck scarf. Casper's got his own scars but nothing like the one's marking Farraday's body who's also present, sitting alongside me to offer his support.

Farraday's always been there when I've got myself in hot water although this is different; I was genuinely trying to help — a point reinforced by Alice, Mae and Fillian who flinch every time Casper adjusts his position.

It was Taeia who commented on his uncle's unwilling-ness to train him and now we know why. The Renns, after all, are water readers, able to assess the temperature of the Society by studying water. The water reader we use in the S.P.M.A. is called a Nivrium — the three silver lines resting on the surface of the water if things are okay, and falling to the bottom if they're not.

No one's brought out a Nivrium yet but Panorilums hover in the moonlit space, Farraday studying one with Philomeena pouring over the other.

"We need to find him quickly," Philomeena states, running her hand over the large piece of parchment, some-thing the adults do when searching for a person in hiding.

Taeia's used the Invisilis charm to hide his movements, but that only works for surveillance devices. I imagine he'll also be hiding behind a protective curtain of light wherever he's gone, but the next comment proves me wrong.

"*There*," comments Farraday, pointing at a familiar building in Society Square: The Blind Horseman.

Taeia isn't stupid enough to go inside, hovering around in the expectation of meeting someone — his faint outline suggesting he's trying to keep himself hidden. Something's forced him out of his protective shell ... a Night Ranger on the run after his mad move on The Hallowed Lawn ... *just when* I thought I'd got through to him.

It was his comment about Casper that seemed to trigger his fury ... the fact his uncle wouldn't train him the source of the massive chip on his shoulder. He'll have more than a grudge to bear if he does anything else stupid, like joining forces with the black market rats heading his way — shifty figures who know better than to get caught up with a wizard on the wanted list.

It's strange to even think those words ... an underage

member never having made the list before, reinforcing the suspicions others had about him. It's not going to do anything to bolster the role of Night Rangers, that's for sure, a thought that seems to be crossing Casper's mind.

"And you suggested the competition to train the others?" Casper prompts, moving his gaze along the outer edge of The Seating Station where the seven of us sit: Night Rangers with a lot of explaining to do.

"Yes, as I've already explained," I reply with a touch of frustration.

"She's not lying, Mr Renn," Fillian adds, braving the wrath of a man that can break him with a move he wouldn't see coming.

I mentioned that Aarav Khan was the only person more intense than Casper Renn, although I didn't add that Aarav isn't on the same level when it comes to advanced sorcery — that's a plane few ever get to and Kaira's dad cruises on it: one of the greatest wizards in the Society's history who's been woken up with stories of a Night Ranger's betrayal. It's fair to say he doesn't seem delighted with the news.

"So, where did it all go wrong?" Philomeena queries, placing her gaze on me.

I can never lie to her — the woman who first took me under her wing after my mum got lost in her quest for power. She's done a *hell of a lot* to protect me, which she's trying to do now, so I need to stick to the facts.

"I honestly don't know," I begin. "One minute we're all laughing after creating a roof of light with the Spintz charms, and the next ... just as we're preparing to guide the others in the art of reaction time ... Taeia loses it and starts punching his Williynx, firing out screaming streaks of light towards me."

"And you didn't say anything to trigger the attack?" Farraday asks, gulping down a vial of Srynx Serum to ease the itching pain of his scars.

"Guppy didn't say anything," Conrad replies, coming to my aid. "It's exactly as she said. We were trying to guide them, explaining they weren't flexible enough in thought, getting caught between ideas in that split-second moment when you have to react."

"And ...?" Farraday prompts, gesturing for further clarity as the faint figure of Taeia Renn disappears on the Panorilum.

"And he nodded," Noah explains, "telling us to get on with it."

"That's it?" Casper challenges, a familiar darkness crossing his face: the mixed-race legend you *don't* want to get on the wrong side of.

"That's it," Lucy adds, "and then he went mental."

"And you concur with this version of events?" Casper continues, stepping closer to Mae, Alice and Fillian who flinch again, knowing full well they're aligned to a wizard on the run — not the position you want to be in with three legendary sorcerers staring down at you.

Mae, Alice and Fillian nod, deciding further explanation might jeopardise their future in the S.P.M.A. It seems to do the trick as Casper flicks open his brass pocket watch to check the time. He's essentially retired from Society duty, leaving the monitoring to less war-weary members, but something tells me he'll be back in action if we don't clean up this mess quickly.

"Well, we find ourselves in a situation," he begins, sitting alongside Fillian who shoots a nervous glance in my direction.

"Scribberals will be rattling soon, Casper," Farraday adds.

"Not if people don't talk," counters Philomeena, as stylish as ever in her blue suit dress. "The only people who know about it are sitting here now, and I doubt Taeia's going to be broadcasting his actions above ground."

"But things could get messy quickly if we don't bring him in soon," Farraday adds.

"Indeed," Casper replies, studying his pocket watch as if the answer's hidden inside.

We're dealing with the adult trio who've saved our lives on more than one occasion, clearly not wanting to get dragged into another battle.

"Twenty-four hours," Casper says finally, standing as he does. "That's the time you've got to bring Taeia in unharmed. If you don't, we review your roles in the Society, beginning with *you three*."

He points at Mae, Alice and Fillian before adding, "I don't believe you're so ignorant to have not noticed the warning signs, yet you've said nothing. Added to which, a group of very powerful people want to make your acquaintance: an action I've put a stop to for now."

The colour drains from the faces of the three we've been competing with tonight, Fillian looking like he's going to be sick. It seems their arrogance isn't going to be enough after all.

"Did you really think you could fire down on your comrades without repercussions?" Farraday adds to reinforce the point of consequences. "Guppy gave you a chance tonight, offering guidance to your idiot captain who decided to mix curses with defensive charms. So, I'm going to ask one question and you'd *better* answer honestly. Has Taeia Renn ever used curses before, even when practicing magic?"

The three of them shake their heads, tears forming in Alice's eyes.

"Never," she says. "I swear. He gets angry but *never*."

"And you two?"

"Never," they repeat.

"We didn't like what he's been doing," Mae adds. "The game of firing down charms on people. They were never going to hurt anybody ... really weak charms like firework displays ... just for fun."

"And if I fired a firework display in your direction now," Philomeena adds, "would you find that fun?"

This shuts them up for good, Fillian joining Alice in the tears department, realising he's going to be sweeping floors if we don't track down Taeia in the next twenty-four hours.

"You three stay with us," Casper states, gesturing for Mae, Fillian and Alice to stand. "You won't return to your own faculty until this is resolved. Let's hope, for your sake, the others can solve this little problem, because if Taeia does *anything* to expose our Society, things won't end well for you."

I suppress a laugh as Fillian breaks wind, crying as he lets rip again. Timing clearly isn't his thing — not in magical competition or choice of friends.

"Farraday will keep an eye on you for now."

"With pleasure," Farraday adds, winking at us as he claps his hands for our frightened foes to follow him. "How many of you know The Cendryll's layout?"

Only Mae nods, not daring to hold Farraday's gaze. It's easy to get lost in the scars marking his face and body, causing you to stare for longer than you should — clearly not the right move to make now.

"Well, lead the way," Farraday adds, clapping again to shock her into action.

As the group head towards the spiral staircase, Casper sits again, leaving only Philomeena standing who speaks first.

"We're aware your intentions were good, Guppy — as they always are — but this doesn't change the fact we've got a loose cannon above ground."

"What do you think he'll do?" Lucy asks, glancing at a blank pamphlet on the floor ... *No News is Good News* ... the name of the Society pamphlet *everyone* wants to stay blank. No news means no drama and although Taeia isn't particularly dangerous, his mouth might be.

"He'll seek shelter with a familiar face," Philomeena states, "saying nothing about his actions on The Hallowed Lawn."

"Any ideas who?" Noah asks.

"A friend who doesn't know him well enough to suspect," Casper adds. "He's a Renn, after all, meaning he'll suspect you've come here to inform us, beginning the formulation of the plan to find him. Luckily, he isn't a popular character, meaning he has few friends above ground. Although, if he is the psychopath I think he is, he may gravitate toward these above-ground characters as a way of threatening us."

"Creating a scene as we close in," I say, "threatening to expose our secret world."

"Precisely, Guppy, so you will need help on this mission."

"You've done enough for us, Casper."

"Not from us. Our role is to oversee all parts of the Society from the inner sanctum of The Cendryll. I also have to keep an eye on Kaira, taking me away from day-to-day business here."

"How is she?" I ask.

"Happy although she misses you all."

"Happy to be out of this, you mean," Conrad adds with a knowing smile.

"There's a time for duty and a time for space," Philomeena adds, glancing at the S.P.M.A. logo on the marble floor washed in moonlight. "Your time will come where space matters more. For now, duty calls: a matter of clearing up a spillage we need to contain."

"We will," Noah says, always quiet around Kaira's dad and aunt.

He doesn't know them as well as Conrad and me, only hearing the stories second hand — of a brother and sister able to create powerful force fields in the blink of an eye.

"You must," Casper adds, buttoning the waistcoat of his dark, blue suit. "Otherwise, those with resentments directed at Night Rangers will be proven right."

"That we can't be trusted," Lucy states.

"Precisely, Lucy. Your loyalty is without question, but that won't help if this story gets out. After all, people hold on to the facts that suit their narrative — that you started another firefight unnecessarily. The fact you were actually on a compassionate mission will count for little, so move with stealth and strike with subtlety, bringing Taeia in *alive* and unharmed. If you go against these conditions, you will only turn suspicion on yourselves. Twenty-four hours. No rest until he's found."

"You mentioned help," I prompt.

"Which will arrive at the appropriate time," Philomeena replies. "A figure appearing recently, offering a vision of the darkness buried within Taeia."

Aarav Khan, I think, not wanting to say it in Noah's presence. I remember Aarav saying how he liked to give his nephew space — the reason he vanished when Noah appeared after his own meeting in the Zilom skies. We've generally outgrown adult guidance, but there are still times when it's necessary.

After all, if Taeia knows he's going to get kicked out, what's stopping him from using magic above ground? It's never been done in plain sight before, mainly because nobody wants to return to the above-ground world once they've tasted this incredible one. Members choose rehabilitation over expulsion, accepting a life as a Melackin where magic is still in reach with the right sponsors.

It's different with Taeia, though, because rehabilitation is never performed on an underage wizard, making his moves harder to predict. I've sort of created this mess so I'm going to put it right, understanding the need to tread carefully.

"Twenty-four hours," Casper repeats, standing from The Seating Station. "Clean up your mess and bring him in."

There isn't a trace of doubt in his voice, making me feel a little better. As I tie up my brown hair, we say our goodbyes to Kaira's dad and aunt.

"Who do you think the mysterious helper is?" Lucy asks.

"Kerevenn," Conrad replies with a smile. "I think he's going to hide behind a lamp post until Taeia pops up."

"He might stand out," I say, going along with the joke. "A giant peering through the top-floor window of The Blind Horsemen."

"Whoever it is, they better be good at tracking ghosts," Lucy states, "because Taeia's a coward at heart so he'll stay in hiding as long as he can."

"We'll have to risk using the Follygrin above ground," I add, uttering 'Comeuppance' to ready the surveillance device for action.

"Another twenty-four hours of fun," Noah says, yawning to make the point he's not looking forward to this.

"Come on," Conrad urges, switching into warrior mode. "Time to track an enemy down."

18

HUNTING ABOVE GROUND

Society Square has an eerie silence … as if it senses a malev in its mist. We study the empty streets inside The Spinning Shoe, a place with its own magical portal to the wonderland of Senreiya. There's no time for wonder at the moment, the four of us looking for any sign of Taeia and the mystery guide arriving to help us. I'm fairly sure it's going to be Aarav Khan, based on Casper's reference to 'a figure offering a vision of the darkness buried within Taeia'.

Either way, it won't matter much if we don't get to Taeia in time … the consequences of him using magic above ground falling on us all. I'm not as worried as Mae, Alice and Fillian who've got Farraday to keep them company — our scarred comrade who'll do his best to scare them into revealing anything else they know.

They were probably telling the truth regarding never witnessing their unstable captain using dark magic before. For their sake, I hope they're not hiding anything.

"We need to move," Conrad suggests, uttering Verum Veras to spread a glittering blanket of protection around us.

The plan is to move unseen along Follyflint Street until we reach Scholar's Court, giving us a perfect vantage point to keep tabs on our new enemy. Part of me wishes Taeia had just *listened*, parking his ego for a few minutes to learn the skills he's never been able to grasp.

Then again, I had no idea of the rage roaring within him — the crazy act of blasting out a blaze of cursed fire about to put an end to his time here. As rehabilitation is never done on underage members, the only punishment left is expulsion.

"I can't see him anywhere," Lucy comments as we move along the empty streets, resting in the faint light illuminating the shop windows.

There are usually a few Society stragglers hanging around at this time — black market rats mainly — but they've got a sense for trouble so have made a swift exit, moving with the changing mood of the evening. Anyone offering Taeia shelter faces a similar fate, suggesting he's probably following the strategy Casper mentioned, hoping to bump into an old above-ground acquaintance who's none the wiser to our secret universe of wonders.

"I doubt he's got many saviours above ground," Noah comments as we huddle up in Scholar's Court, the cool evening breeze running over my skin.

It's times like these that I think a jacket would be of benefit, but my uniform of black, leather trousers and matching top has become part of my 'look' as Conrad likes to call it, currently on a mission to appease a troubled soul.

"Who does he know above ground?" Lucy queries, getting a shrug from us as we keep our eyes on activity in The Blind Horseman.

The ground floor of the pub is the above-ground section, but non-magical folk have long vacated, leaving the secret space on the top floor still buzzing with activity. Some members barely sleep, managing magic in the day and their choice of remedies at night.

I doubt any of them will help a wizard on the run but, then again, the decision's been made not to broadcast Taeia's mad moment, making me consider something else — if Casper's got something else other than expulsion in mind.

Compared to how fast sleeping soldiers were sent on the hunt for Odin and Neve Blin, there's no such urgency where Taeia's concerned. This could be because he's underage or, maybe, because the Society elders don't want to make this worse than it already is. It would just be easier to swarm the square with sleeping soldiers, making it impossible for the lost boy in question to be captured.

Instead, the burden falls on our shoulders because of my decision to offer a guiding hand. I suppose Taeia's never bought into the 'beauty and unity' idea we all live by, leaving the question of his punishment in the hands of the Society elders. First, we've got to find him in time.

"I say we go in," I suggest. "Head up to the second floor to see if he's there."

"Sounds like a plan," Conrad replies. "It beats standing out here in the cold."

"He's not stupid enough to head up there, is he?" Noah asks. "Knowing he's being tracked, I mean."

"Where else can he go?" I challenge. "He might be looking for above-ground friends, but they're all fast asleep. The only option he's got is to lie low until the morning when he can ease his way into the crowd, maintaining methods of invisibility."

"Increases our chances of losing him," Lucy adds. "We've got less than twenty-four hours to find him or *we're* in trouble — so much for helping a lost soul."

"Which is my fault."

"It's no-one's fault," Conrad counters. "You did the right thing, following our Society's principles of peace over conflict. We tried and failed, but that's less to do with us than it is with Taeia's demons."

"Which doesn't change the fact we've got a problem if we don't find him," Noah states, rubbing his hands within our protective curtain of light. "Anyway, I'm getting cold and need a drink so let's head inside. If he isn't there, we grab a drink. If he is ... well ... we'll see how *that* plays out."

"No more cursed fire, hopefully," Lucy comments as we exit Scholar's Court, turning the corner to the establishment in question.

"If only he'd *listened*," Conrad whispers to me, maybe sharing the same sense of regret I'm feeling. The essence of Night Ranging is to keep to the peace, avoiding situations like this one. I don't get any pleasure from capturing comrades, viewing it as a sign of ongoing instability. Not like it was before, obviously, but each new capture suggests we're storing up bigger problems.

"Time for a drink," I say, sensing our target isn't where we're headed but, instead, watching us from one of the buildings resting in the evening light. Looks like we're in for another long night.

WE MAKE OUR WAY TO THE UPPER FLOOR OF THE BLIND Horsemen, using the Entrinias charm to enter through the 'Staff Only' door. Once locked, we enter one of the empty toilet cubicles acting as a Perium. The back wall of each cubicle has a smaller door, leading to another room twice the size of the rest of the building.

Only half of the oak tables are occupied, those conditioned to hanging out in the midnight hours hunched over their favourite remedies. There's no sign of Taeia or any other underage witch or wizard, The Blind Horsemen not a typical hideout for the young. The clientele has been of the shifty kind until recently — Alice Aradel a case in point.

The evening witch used the place as her trading base, drawing desperate people into bargains they'd end up paying heavily for. This included Society members and above-ground folk alike, all looking for a solution to their problems. The more desperate they got, the more they were prepared to do until things got out of hand.

We're not going *there* again, meaning we'll need all our wit and skill to work out where Taeia's hiding. He's not going to put himself in the firing line so the only places left are quiet ones, like the buildings lining Society Square and Founders' Quad.

Where would an underage hideout when things had gone haywire?

"I'll get the drinks," Noah says, heading to the empty bar and the twitchy wizard tapping his head to stay awake.

"We need to narrow down potential hideouts," I suggest, running my hand over the S.P.M.A. logo carved into the oak table.

"I'll make a list," Lucy offers, enacting the Canvia charm so she can draw on the table. "Fire away."

"Tallis & Crake," I begin. "The trading lane hidden inside — not the shop. No one stays up there at night and it's got four access points."

"Good one, Guppy," Conrad adds "although what if he's already left The Society Sphere?."

"He's here," I say. "He's never strayed too far, mainly because he knows the limitations of his powers."

"He'd also expect to be swarmed by a Society army if he did," Lucy adds. "I agree with Guppy. He'll choose somewhere familiar where he can keep an eye on things, and us."

"Think high up," Noah states, returning with a tray of drinks: Liqin for tonight's errand. "He'll want a vantage point to see everything. A ground floor space won't give him that, limiting the places he can access."

"Because a lot of higher floors are occupied by shop owners," Conrad adds, following Noah's train of thought.

"So, Tallis & Crake," Lucy says, writing the name of the shop in citrine light which hovers above the table. "Where else has accessible space on the upper floors?"

"Helping Hand," I reply, remembering heading there after my first experience of Dyil's Ditch, and the vampiric birds that tried to attack me.

"Zucklewick's," Noah adds. "Ivo lets people use the second floor sometimes."

"Taeia wouldn't risk Zucklewick's," Conrad suggests. "Ivo knows everything that happens in the Society, including things he's not supposed to."

"The Sylent...?" Lucy suggests in a whispered voice, choosing not to add this name to the list of glowing letters decorating the oak table.

"He wouldn't," Noah says, frowning at the thought of it.

"Why wouldn't he? If he thinks he's going to be kicked out, why wouldn't he go to a building with a dark history?"

"So, where do we start?" I prompt, sipping my Liqin as a group of weary wizards head for the exit.

"Familiar territory," Conrad replies. "The place Taeia's most comfortable in, giving him a chance of escape if he's found."

"The trading lane of Tallis & Crake," I suggest. "I always saw him there, trading basic artefacts for more complex ones. It also gives him an edge because if he stays out of sight, we'll be walking into his firing line."

"We've got to bring him in unharmed, remember?" Lucy prompts, holding my gaze to make sure I'm not planning another duel.

"Which will be tricky if he's on the war path," I reply.

"He hasn't got battle in his soul," Conrad states matter-of-factly, gulping down his Liqin before standing. "Come on. Time to check out Tallis & Crake."

19

SHADOW STRIKE

Tallis & Crake sits in darkness, the shop known for its secret trading lane displaying more traditional goods in the shop window. Two wall lamps maintain the permanent, dull glow inside, illuminating the Gothic feel of the place. The 'Staff Only' door is the place we're headed to and, more specifically, what lies behind it. The Verum Veras charm is still active, keeping us hidden from prying eyes.

No one's walking the midnight streets but you never know who's watching. It's important to stay hidden on the off chance Taeia *is* hiding out in the trading lane. With the 'Staff Only' door closed behind us, we squeeze into the small, square space lined with mirrors on each side.

Kneeling to keep our balance as our mode of transport picks up pace, I study the mirrors that offer no reflection — a seemingly pointless feature until you realise you can fall through them, landing face first on the trading lane. Tallis & Crake was the first place I thought of after guessing Taeia had got off the streets, heading for a more isolated spot. It's perfect because of the darkness it lies in at night, including the fact it isn't supervised.

If things *do* get out of hand, I'm sure Ina Tallis will turn up to shut things down. Ina runs the shop below, thinking nothing of tying annoying comrades in knots to keep the peace. After all, it's her job to keep up appearances above ground. We'll only see Ina if our mystery helper doesn't arrive first, my money still on Aarav Khan.

"Here we go," Noah whispers as the mirrors fade away, offering a vision of the trading lane.

It's a long, rectangular space marked by four diagonal walkways that lead onto it. Normally, there's a queue on each of the walkways but trades only take place in the day — not your typical trading, of course. You sit on a stool on the trading lane, placing the artefact you want to trade in the wooden drawer. You then sit and wait, hoping the drawer pops open with the hoped-for artefact.

Sometimes you get what you want and sometimes you don't, heading to the bartering boxes if things don't go to plan. It's not the most obvious place to hide out in, but when your options are limited it makes perfect sense. The vaulted ceiling lacks light, creating a space of shadows ... the only shapes visible the stools and wooden panelling decorating the trading lane.

"I say we separate," I suggest, "each entering on a different walkway."

"Minimising the target and multiplying the threat," Lucy adds, liking the idea.

"Let's do it," Conrad says, rolling his neck as we step through different sections of our small chamber, taking us onto different ends of the four walkways leading to the central lane.

Invisibility is key now, particularly as we're following

orders to bring Taeia in unharmed. I occupy the west walkway, activating a tornado of blue light around me, ready to step into the firing line if need be. Conrad glimmers into view momentarily, signalling his position wrapped in a black web that morphs to the shape of his body: the Weveris charm that can shield, sink and trap.

With Noah and Lucy staying out of sight, we move along our walkways slowly, listening out for any sound in the unsettling silence. Energy will reveal Taeia if he's here ... another advanced trait I picked up in my early days. Invisibility is a weapon you need to protect against, like all other forms of defence. It's a point I tried to make on The Hallowed Lawn but Taeia had other ideas — ideas that have brought us here.

The first sound comes from the end of the trading lane ... a clattering sound that echoes in the space. A wisp of yellow light appears on the east walkway in the colour of Lucy's penchant stone ... light that floats to the floor before it runs towards the source of the sound. Someone's here so we ready ourselves to engage with the target ... stealth and subtlety required to avoid another 'incident'.

The light released by Lucy darts in various directions along the central lane, rising along the east wall shrouded in darkness. No figure shows themselves until I hear Lucy whisper 'Exhibius', revealing the shaking figure of Taeia Renn, looking lost in a space that can't save him. As broken as he seems, I remember the fury in his face when he lost control on The Hallowed Lawn. Insecure and volatile, he's a bundle of nervous energy likely to explode into action at any moment.

"Easy, Taeia," Conrad offers, deactivating the Verum Veras charm to reveal himself, masked in a black web.

I'm not sure Conrad's chosen the most reassuring look, but I understand we can't afford to take chances.

"Let's just talk," Conrad adds, stepping onto the trading lane with his hands raised in a sign of co-operation.

"Talk about what?" Taeia barks, crouched in the corner framed by Lucy's yellow light. "It's *over*. I've *messed up* like everyone knew I would."

"It's not as bad as you think," I add, lying through my teeth. "No one got hurt."

A bitter laugh echoes through the trading lane. "I tried to use a *curse*, Grayling. A mixture of dark and light magic that no one's going to forgive. I *can't* go to The Velynx."

"You're not going to The Velynx," Lucy replies as we all appear on our walkways, decorated in various forms of protection, Lucy choosing a simple Velinis charm for maximum transparency.

"Of *course* I'm going to The Velynx."

"You're *not*," Noah states, surrounded by circles of fire. "Underage members have never been sent there."

"I'm sure they'll make an exception for me."

"Why did you do it, Taeia?" I ask, trying to keep his mind off the place for bad things and bad people. "We were trying to help you."

"In front of my crew, making me look like a half-witted wizard."

"Better than where we are now," Conrad adds, inching forwards on the trading lane. "Now we've got a situation."

"Bringing me in," Taeia states, standing up from his crouched position.

"Yes."

"So, where am I going if I'm not being sent to The Velynx?"

"That's up to the adults."

"You're *lying!*" he shouts, pivoting suddenly, sending a ball of morphing steel flying towards the stools closest to him. The steel smashes into the stools ... the splintering wood floating towards our lost comrade ... another sign of his darkening intentions. "There's *no way* you don't know what's going to happen to me so spill it or take your chances."

"The only chance you've got is coming in with us," Noah replies, activating a force field of light in front of us, joining forces on the trading lane. "That's the truth."

"And what chance would that be...? Life as a Melackin."

"Not done on underage members."

"Kicked out, then."

"Maybe," I add, "unless you make it worse by doing something stupid now."

"I say we go out with a bang, Grayling. You know, putting your Fire Witch status to the test."

"Take it easy, Taeia," I urge, understanding the consequences of this backfiring. "Just come in with us so we can sort things out."

"There's nothing to sort out," comes the reply from a lost boy about to abandon a life of magical allegiance. "Let's dance."

The force field surrounding us will be enough to quell any initial fire, but there's no fun in hiding in battle so I prepare to make light work of Taeia's final stand. Chaos isn't easy to control, particularly when your only experience of battle is firing down on unsuspecting comrades, so I point my right hand to the vaulted ceiling, ready to add my own touch to tonight's action.

A rain of splintered wood blasts towards us, courtesy of another group of smashed stools destroyed by our new foe, but the Fora charm takes care of this — the force field halting all momentum. We could end the evening like this, walking forwards behind the protective shield until Taeia runs out of options. He hasn't worked out that Lucy's frame of light stops him from escaping ... a simple twist of the wrist turning into a shrinking force field, preventing all forms of magical transport.

We'll see how long it takes him to work this out as he strides forward, wiping away his tears as he blasts out balls of light that explode inches from us ... not enough to penetrate our Fora charm. If anything, our lack of retaliation is making him angrier, shouting 'Let's go!' each time he tries to do damage. His magical hourglass is running out and he knows it, firing blindly until I decide it's time to shut him up.

Whispering 'Disineris', I clench my fist to explode the vaulted ceiling, directing the falling fragments towards our fading enemy who ducks, whipping out shields of light and energy just in time. He hasn't got the imagination to be a warrior, not working out that a simple adjustment re-directs the falling debris ... now formed into arrows darting ... the force of the attack making him lose his balance.

Stranded and desperate, he tries the obvious, shouting 'DISIRA' but Lucy's kept him framed within the shrinking forcefield of light ... the four of us moving forwards slowly, controlling the direction of the collapsing ceiling to make sure no damage is done.

"Let me go!" Taeia shouts in desperation, writhing on the floor as we reach him.

"The time for squealing is over," I say, my compassion for his cause fading fast.

"We need to tidy up," Noah suggests, working with Lucy to repair the ceiling while Conrad keeps an eye on me.

He knows me well enough to recognise the warning signs — an old volatility rising to the surface.

"It's done, Guppy," Conrad states. "We've done as instructed: no injuries."

I nod, kicking away the shower of splinters around Taeia's stranded frame. "To think we fought so hard for cretins like him to be allowed entry."

"It's *done*, Guppy. Leave it."

I step back as Taeia tries to kick out at me, grimacing as the pain of the Fixilia charm kicks in.

"You're always going to have bad eggs, Guppy; it's human nature."

"Well, this bad egg's stinking the place out. Let's get him back to The Cendryll."

Noah and Lucy join us, glancing up to check the ceiling's been fully restored.

"Looks good," I say, referring to their restoration job.

"All my work," Noah teases, getting a gentle nudge from Lucy. "So, what happened to our mystery helper? Wasn't he supposed to arrive in our moment of need?"

"Not needed in the end," Lucy replies, adjusting the hair clip in her cropped, black bob.

"It's weird that Casper made a thing of it," Noah continues, "as if he'd orchestrated it."

"He's always been a man of mystery," Conrad adds before adding, "Speaking of a man of mystery, who's that...?"

We turn to catch sight of a silhouetted figure standing at the end of the west walkway, dressed immaculately in a pin-striped black suit ... dark-skinned and bald headed ... hovering inches from the ground.

"My uncle," Noah replies, not looking all that happy to see him, "coming to the rescue too late again."

I decide to leave that comment hanging, hoping to avoid another family drama.

"Glad you could make it!" Noah shouts, kicking Taeia in

the shoulder as he tries to move again. "Two bloody divas in one room," he mutters, jaw clenched as if he's biting down on his anger.

With one diva out of action and another hovering in silence, I get ready to reacquaint myself with Aarav Khan — the mystic figure I met in the skies of Zilom, arriving to conclude tonight's events.

20

SAVING GRACE

Aarav Khan spends the first few minutes staring up at the ceiling, inspecting Noah and Lucy's work. I initially think this is something he does when his nephew's present, checking on the quality of Noah's wizardry. It's certainly having the desired effect — Conrad, Lucy and I sharing puzzled glances while Noah seethes in silence.

"Everything restored to its rightful place," Aarav comments after what feels like an endless pause.

"What were you expecting, a bomb site," Noah replies, falling into what seems like a familiar rhythm.

It must be difficult having a relative who's a legend. I've got some experience of this although my mum's of the infamous kind. This is different — this thing between Noah and Aarav — a familiar game of to-and-fro that amuses the mysterious wizard and annoys the hell out of his nephew.

"So, you're the mysterious helper," I say, thinking I should break up the family reunion.

"Indeed, Guppy. It's good to see you again."

"You know each other?" Lucy queries, flinching every time Aarav does another spin.

It would be fair to say he's a bit dramatic, making me understand where Noah's 'diva' comment comes from. There's a lot more to him, though, specifically the intense energy he gives off almost hypnotic in its power. You can't fail to be drawn to a man dressed immaculately and acting mysteriously, as if he's a puzzle we're supposed to solve.

"We met in Zilom," I explain to the others. "Aarav was my guide. He showed me an image using a Now-Then: a past image involving Taeia's crew and what they were up to."

"A vision that brought us here," Noah's uncle comments, spinning again but this time turning his attention to our captured comrade. "To a boy drowning in his own self-pity."

Taeia attempts to spit at Aarav which doesn't turn out well for him ... the mystic magician uttering an incantation I don't catch which lifts Taeia to his feet. The way he rises is uncomfortable to watch ... his skin stretching around his face and body as if he's being pierced with an invisible thread. Whatever sorcery he's using makes Taeia grimace in pain: punishment for a foul mouth.

"Dignity and decorum are two things which have bypassed you," Aarav states, stepping closer to Taeia's figure forced into an upright position in a strange vision of crucifixion.

It doesn't feel right, but who am I to question a man put on my path by Farraday? Also, Kerevenn was our guide to Zilom and Casper said we'd meet someone tonight, so this must be all part of the plan as uncomfortable as it is to watch.

"Is that really necessary?" Lucy asks. "The Fixilia charm was doing just fine."

"I prefer variety in all things magical," Aarav replies,

resting his gaze on Lucy momentarily. "One of the reasons I've been chosen for tonight's adventure."

"To torture a kid," Noah quips with evident sarcasm.

"The pain your fallen comrade feels is no greater than having your skin pinched."

"He's clearly in more pain than that," Conrad challenges, stepping back as Aarav turns his attention on him. "I'm just saying I agree with Lucy; it doesn't seem necessary."

"Although you haven't asked *why*, Conrad."

"Okay, why?"

"To avenge an action considered a sin in our world."

"Attacking a Williynx," I reply instinctively.

Aarav nods, adding, "As sharp as ever, Guppy. Yes, to rebalance things. Williynx are a particularly rare species; a white Williynx the rarest of them all. What Taeia did in punching his feathered companion must be atoned for, this being the opening phase of that atonement."

"He had a chance at redemption on The Hallowed Lawn: a chance he didn't take."

"In a game of your making, Guppy. The rules have changed now due to the situation we find ourselves in. We have an underage malev who can neither be rehabilitated nor imprisoned in The Velynx."

"So, we expel him," Noah states.

His uncle turns to him, spinning elegantly as he does so. The black, pin-striped suit is matched with a blue shirt and tie, the cravat finishing off the look of a wealthy banker. He's rich in others way, obviously, one of them being the secret he's yet to share about a lost boy's future. With Taeia's flesh stretching off his athletic frame, I'm keen to get to the bottom of Aarav's statement to avoid witnessing what *does* look like torture.

"After a meeting with The Orium Circle, a different direction has been decided."

"Which is?" Conrad poses.

"Redemption or retribution on The Hallowed Lawn."

"Bloody hell," Noah comments. "You've turned up to invite us to another game of Rucklz?"

"Sarcasm has its place, Noah, but not in situations such as this."

"Then *spit it out*, uncle. What's the plan?"

"For our fallen comrade to face his Williynx."

"*What*?" the four of us say in unison.

"Why would he get another chance?" Conrad challenges.

"Why did your father get another chance?"

A point that makes Conrad back down. If there's been a meeting with The Orium Circle — the most senior figures in the Society — I bet Casper and Philomeena were there. They've obviously used their famed compassion, convincing the lawmakers to give Taeia one more shot at atonement. Maybe part of it is Casper's guilt in not offering to train his nephew.

Then again, maybe it's a recognition that kicking him back into the above-ground world won't solve the problem. The S.P.M.A. exists in plain sight, after all, hiding within normality. It's the natural development of centuries of magical living, some families not wanting to choose between one or the other, meaning Taeia needs to be managed in a different way.

"Can we stop your display of power now," Noah states, getting what he hopes for as his uncle relents, returning our fallen comrade to a static position trapped in the power of the Fixilia charm.

"So, when is it happening?" Lucy asks, watching as Taeia

rubs the marks covering his skin. "This duel with a Williynx?"

"Now," Aarav replies, decorating the west wall of the trading lane with a flood of light — another dramatic gesture providing a vision of The Hallowed Lawn. It isn't empty this time ... crowds filling stands formed of glittering, orange light: a chamber for a sacrificial gladiator.

"After you," Noah's uncle states, gesturing for us to leave Taeia to him.

None of us argue, following the line of light as we step into a familiar space buzzing with noise.

"This feels weird," I whisper, catching sight of Farraday in the top stand.

"Tell me about it," Conrad adds. "What was the point of sending us to capture the idiot, knowing they were going to give him a second chance?"

"Maybe the mission was our chance to put things right," Lucy suggests.

"Well, we've proven ourselves now so let's enjoy the show," Noah comments, heading for the empty chairs to our right until Lucy grabs hold of him.

"*Enjoy the show*?" she queries, gripping his arm. "An underage member could be on the verge of being obliterated and you want to get popcorn?"

"No way are the Society elders going to allow that."

"Then what's the big stadium for? And the crowds of Society elders?"

"Witches and wizards seeking revenge maybe," I add, sharing Lucy's sinking feeling. "We need to get to Farraday ... this way."

We walk around the boundary of the Rucklz pitch, glancing back to see the broken figure of Taeia Renn floating in the air under Aarav Khan's control. It's public humiliation, all right, and I hope that's all it is because if the skin-stretching's anything to go by, expulsion won't be needed.

WE FIND FARRADAY PERCHED ON THE TOP ROW OF THE stadium, facing North. He waves us towards him, saying 'budge along' to the surrounding people. Tapping the benches, he produces vials of Semphul — the hunger remedy — before he gets us to huddle together, ready to explain the mad vision of a brutal duel with an enraged Williynx.

There's no white-feathered creature in sight yet which sort of makes me feel better, but the glamour added to the occasion suggests the stakes have been raised: the question is how high?

"What's going on, Farraday?" I ask our scar-ravaged friend.

He seems more preoccupied with the handful of pies he's got in a bag by his feet. "Creative consequences," he says through a mouthful of food. "Casper's idea."

"*Casper's* idea?" Conrad queries, unable to process the statement. "Pitting Taeia against the Williynx he punched in the head?"

"Yep."

"Have you all gone mad?"

"All will be explained as we go along, my friend," Farraday replies, offering us a pie which we all accept. "The first thing to understand is that a price must be paid: a price acceptable to one of the rarest creatures in our magical world. Punching any Williynx is bad enough, but attacking *a white Williynx* ... that's a whole different ball game.

We've spent the last few hours trying to calm Oweyna, but no luck. This is the only way to re-earn our feathered friend's trust unless, of course, you want a furious army of Williynx flying in from Gilweean. If we'd refused, our centuries-old allegiance would have been permanently damaged."

"For punching *one* Williynx?" Noah queries.

"*Never* done before and *never to happen again*," Farraday replies with blunt force. "A *disgrace* staining our world."

I decide to nibble on the pie, realising there's no shifting Farraday when he's in this mood. I was hoping to persuade him to intervene but history dictates otherwise. Taeia's crossed more than one line tonight and this one comes at a rare price.

"So, what happens if Taeia can't defend himself?" I ask, hoping I don't hear the answer I dread.

"That's up to our feathered friend."

"Can she kill him?"

"Kill. Maim. Obliterate," Farraday explains, swallowing the last pie whole. "You don't mess with a white Williynx."

"What are the chances of him getting out alive?" Conrad asks.

"Everything depends of Oweyna's ability to forgive. If she makes it easy for him, she disgraces her species. If she murders him, she'll put a stain on the Williynx forever. It will be a lesson no-one will forget: the one solution Casper's convinced The Orium Circle of."

"Are The Orium Circle here?" Lucy asks.

Farraday points to the stands on the opposite side. "On the middle row, looking like they'd rather be somewhere else. Once again, Casper's worked his magic. I just hope Oweyna shares his compassion."

"And if it *is* just a lesson?" Noah prompts.

"Then the lessons continue, according the Casper's lead: the education he refused Taeia on his entrance to the Society. Casper feels responsible, aware of the vacuum in his nephew that will bruise more than a Williynx's pride. Taeia needs to be tamed before he sinks into an empty chasm, leading to problems for us all."

"So, contain the danger within," I comment.

"Precisely, Guppy," Farraday replies as a roar fills the stadium, sending a shiver through me.

"Come on, Taeia," I say, getting an odd look from Conrad. "It could be *my mum* or *your dad*. Who would you be siding with then?"

Conrad retreats, taking my hand as he does so. "You're right," he whispers, adding, "Let's just pray he gets out of this alive."

21

FEATHER FOR A FRIEND

I sit in between Conrad and Farraday as another roar rips through the air. Fear isn't my thing but that doesn't make me immune to the suffering of others. As idiotic as Taeia has been, this is extreme even for Casper. The son of a legendary wizard who engaged with darkness himself, Casper's got a thing about catching malevs before they form into dangerous wizards.

Taeia's in no danger of being great so he's unlikely to pose a significant threat but, then again, it was only a few hours ago that I thought he might be misunderstood. Still, pitting an unskilled wizard against a fierce creature about to spit its fury in his face is *way over the top.*

Taeia's got no chance so there must be something else going on. We're a peaceful Society, after all, not a principle we can maintain if an underage Night Rider gets ripped to pieces in a public execution. Casper's up to something and Farraday knows exactly what it is, but he's more preoccupied with his pies so I lean forward, keeping hold of Conrad's hand as a vision appears.

"Here we go," Farraday says, gulping down a vial of

Srynx Serum. "Do or die."

"You're up to something," I say, giving Farraday the look that normally makes him spill the beans, but he's not biting.

"From what I hear, it's *you lot* who've been up to something, winding up Taeia's crew out here earlier. What made you think a tournament you couldn't lose was going to build his fragile confidence?"

"So it's our fault?" Conrad queries, applying some magical eyedrops as he does: Crilliun for night vision.

"It's no one's fault, Conrad, but it wasn't your best play. Taeia's got a hole in him that can't be filled with magic or mayhem."

"Because he's a Renn?" Noah asks, finishing off his pie.

"No," Farraday replies, "because he's a lost soul, falling for the idea of a magical existence without asking if it suited him."

"And this is the punishment?" Lucy prompts.

"More of a lesson," Farraday replies, burping loudly as he wipes his mouth. "We all know the endless magic Williynx possess. They taught Conrad to free fall, after all."

"So, Oweyna's here to *teach* Taeia?" I ask, getting a bit lost in Farraday's convoluted explanation of things.

"In a way, Guppy: a lesson he's never going to forget, assuming he survives, that is."

As Oweyna — the white Williynx in question — touches down on the centre of The Hallowed Lawn, I turn my attention to Taeia who stands on the furthest boundary, looking terrified. If I could help him I would, but that would only add to our problems: Night Rangers dishonouring executive decisions. The only thing I can do now is pray which I do quietly.

Conrad places an arm around my waist, seeing how much I'm struggling with this. I still can't get my head around Casper choosing this over expulsion. Who benefits from a disastrous outcome? The Society elders, leaving the stadium satisfied a rogue comrade has been put in his place? Casper reasserting his authority in The Cendryll?

"*Jesus!*" Noah yells as the brutal duel begins, Oweyna firing off with a blade of ice that rips through the pitch, racing under the earth towards Taeia's frozen figure.

"Move!" I shout, gesturing for him to activate the flight charm.

"*Sit*, Guppy," Farraday orders but I brush him off, offering the glare he knows too well.

"If you want to watch an execution, fine, but I remember fighting for beauty and unity not long ago and *this isn't it*."

Taeia heeds my advice, propelling himself into the air as the blade of ice bursts out of the earth and into the air … racing towards him as he swings his body in desperation … the propeller motion of the flower struggling to match the speed of the ice blade.

"Destroy it!" I shout again, sensing eyes turning on me but I couldn't care less. Whatever this is, it's wrong so I fight against the principles I live and die by.

With Conrad standing alongside me, equally disgusted by the spectacle, we do our best to sign the necessary counter moves to Taeia, ignoring the hum of the crowd filling the stadium of light. They can whisper their disapproval but I'm not living with this on my conscience, re-employing the compassion and guidance I got wrong earlier.

I can see that inviting Taeia's crew to a game of Rucklz was the wrong move. Like Farraday said, they couldn't win so all it did was reinforce their sense of inadequacy. As Oweyna shape shifts into a massive form, its wing span touching the roof of the stadium of light, I get the feeling the real lesson is about to begin ... the bruise around our feathered friend's eye visible ... a mark of dishonour it wants to avenge.

"He can't use counter fire so he's got no chance," Lucy states as Noah covers his eyes, unable to watch the sight of Oweyna spinning into attack.

The sight of a Williynx blasting towards you is a memorable one, usually because it normally signals the end. I perch on the edge of my seat as Taeia scrambles to protect himself with a Velinis charm — a purple bubble of light that will only keep him safe for a few minutes.

He's only got two options now ... an unauthorised attack or submission ... or so I think until he does something *crazy*, deactivating the Velinis charm as Oweyna closes in. As the white Williynx nears, Taeia tries to *leap on*! It's the worst possible insult after attacking the creature earlier, leading to a free fall of a different kind: a vision of fury roaring towards the shattered earth with a terrified comrade smothered in its feathers.

"She's going to crash land him!" Noah shouts. "Farraday, bloody *do* something!"

"You know the rules of the game," is all we get in reply.

"A Williynx killing its own kind?" I challenge, mildly disgusted with a man a think so much of.

"No longer our own kind and about to sink into the earth," Farraday replies with a strange coldness, leaving me with only one option: a vanishing towards the eye of the storm. Someone beats me to it, though ... *Jacob* ... appearing out of nowhere ... lying face up on The Hallowed Lawn in the direct flight path of the roaring Williynx ... a sight that leaves me speechless and brings the crowds to their feet.

I KNOW I'M TOO LATE NOW ... UNABLE TO WATCH THE CLOSING moments ... yelling in fury at the sound of Taeia's screams. I grip Conrad's hand, engulfed by the silence that follows. I expect to see a bloodbath when I open my eyes, knowing if I do the Society's dead to me. A familiar squawk gives me a sliver of hope — the squawk of acceptance all Williynx offer when allegiance has been formed.

When I open my eyes, I see Taeia lying face down on the ground near Jacob's feet, looking like he's about to grab on to my brother for dear life.

"What happened?" I ask.

"A saviour arrived," Farraday replies with a smile, suggesting he knew about this all along.

"So, this whole stadium thing was just to scare Taeia?"

"And provide a public test."

"For who?"

"The young. The Society elders have been moaning about underage members, so we thought a bit of night time drama would put them straight. Obviously, we knew you'd play your part, ready to intervene before Jacob added the finishing touches. Sometimes, adults need to be reminded of the power of the young ... exactly what Jacob's doing now."

"Jacob knew about this?" I ask, annoyed he didn't mention anything to me.

"He knew his part," Farraday adds cryptically, "and now he just needs to add the finishing touches."

Everyone in the stadium remains on their feet, enraptured by the sight of something rare: a wizard with the power to stop a Williynx's fury. Jacob's got a special connection with Society creatures, calling them in ways I've never understood.

My brother lies on the ground as Oweyna taps him with

her white beak — as if they're talking in a strange language. Jacob blinks each time he's prodded, stroking the white feathers standing on end: a sign Taeia's not out of the woods yet.

"Jacob needs to get Taeia to safety," Conrad says, leaning over the barrier of the stadium of light. "It doesn't look like Oweyna's forgiven the punch in the head."

"Jacob knows what he's doing," I state, remembering how he turned the Quij into a fire-red army. "He's a creature tamer of a different sort almost knowing the secret language of each magical species, connecting with them on a level no one else can."

"I don't think making out with a Williynx means you know what you're doing," Noah jokes.

"You could always lend a hand," Lucy counters, nudging Noah forward from our high vantage point. "You know, show Jacob how it's done."

"I couldn't leave my Princess on her own."

"Don't worry," Lucy replies with a sarcastic smile. "I'm sure I'll find a new frog."

This brings a laugh to proceedings, helping to ease the tension. It's also good to see Jacob getting to his feet, arms placed around Oweyna's neck: a symbol he's talked her down from smashing Taeia to pieces. Jacob's voice breaks the silence — a call of "kneel" to Taeia who does just that.

With our lost boy adopting a position of submission, my brother directs the head of the white Williynx towards Taeia, rubbing its neck as he does so. Jacob blows on his hands, releasing a cloud of dust around Oweyna. I've never seen this trick before, guessing it's healing by design, trying to repair the bond between wizard and Williynx Taeia did his best to break.

"He's got one chance," Farraday comments, running a

hand through his thinning mop of hair. "If he flinches, he's done for."

"He won't," I reply, trusting my brother's healing touch.

Let's face it, it's Jacob who persuaded me to forgive mum after what she did. He's a healer by nature, probably the reason he's fallen into teaching. He was my teacher for a long time in many ways, helping to fix my mistakes and heal my wounds. I miss him loads and wish we could spend more time together, but he's got different people to save now.

As Oweyna's beak rests on Taeia's head, I spot Casper for the first time, stepping onto The Hallowed Lawn: the conductor of tonight's ceremony. Without speaking to Jacob, Casper sends a streak of light into the air — an act copied by every adult in the stadium, leaving the four of us to join in.

"What are we doing?" Conrad asks.

"Setting the pace," Farraday replies with a smile. "Taeia's about to go on the ride of his life."

"So, he's been forgiven?"

"In a way, but now he's got to prove he's sorry."

"How?" I ask.

"By surviving the joy ride," Farraday says, laughing as he glances at the cascade of light. "Let's just say Taeia's in for a *long* night."

I watch Oweyna streak into the sky, her white wings expanding before she releases a feather which floats down towards Jacob. It's the peace offering of the evening: a sign no permanent damage has been done.

The S.P.M.A. works in strange ways sometimes and the reasons aren't always clear, but I'm happy that what looked like a public execution has turned into an important lesson. We'll find out Taeia's fate soon enough but, for now, I just want my bed and a certain boy wizard in it.

22

MANAGING MALICE

We head to the ground floor of The Cendryll after a broken night of sleep, Conrad's restless energy keeping me up most of the night: not in *that* way. Conrad's got a bee in his bonnet about Taeia's fate, arguing that it needs to be fair or our problems with some of the Society elders will continue. I argue that fair's a relative term. It wasn't exactly fair that my mum was taken to a hideout after her mistake.

Equally, Conrad's dad got special treatment when his loose tongue got us all in trouble — the start of the mayhem a few years ago. Then there was my mad dash to Dyil's Ditch which almost got a lot of people killed. The decision will be less about fairness and more about justice, a statement that annoys Conrad even more.

"How are they different things?" he challenges as we cross The Floating Floor.

Strictly speaking, we're not allowed to spend the night together since we're still underage wizards. Our take on things is that sixteen is the accepted age for a lot of things so, as long as we're discreet, a night-time cuddle isn't doing anyone any harm.

"One's about perception and the other's about the options," I reply in relation to our fairness / justice debate. "It wasn't fair that I was allowed a second chance after chasing a shifty witch to Dyil's Ditch. The reason I got away with it was because my intentions were good, sensing Cialene Koll was an important piece of the puzzle."

"But Taeia's intentions *weren't* good," Conrad counters, "which is my whole point. I get he's too young to get the Melackin treatment or be parked in The Velynx but *why* help him beyond that? Because we're worried he'll cause havoc above ground?"

"Which he undoubtedly would."

"So, keeping our enemies close."

"Maybe ... and guilt partly," I suggest, struggling with a splitting headache. "At the end of the day, Casper knows what he's doing so we're going to have to trust him."

"Meaning...?"

"Meaning maybe Taeia resents his uncle's choice, causing him to carry that massive chip on his shoulder. You could say it's the ultimate embarrassment: a Renn who's unskilled in wizardry and ignored by his powerful relatives. If he receives the proper training, it might divert him from the dark path Aarav's convinced he's on."

"So, you think it's the right choice?"

"I think it's the *only* choice and if Casper thinks the same, that's fine by me."

We reach the spiral staircase, seeing no sign of activity below.

"As long as we don't have to babysit him anymore."

"I just want to know why we've been woken up so early,

our Scribberal rattling like an alarm clock at *five* this morning."

"Urgent business, probably," Conrad replies, rubbing his face in attempt to stay alert.

"Not too urgent to stop me going back to bed afterwards. I don't think I've slept properly for six months."

"It's all that dangerous living," Conrad jokes, nudging me gently.

"Maybe Kaira had the right idea, going off travelling."

"There's nothing stopping us doing the same thing."

"Sooner rather than later," I say at the sight of the lift descending towards the ground floor, "before we're too old or too scarred."

"To places we've never been to before," Conrad mutters with a smile.

"Deal," I say, raising a hand to Casper and Philomeena who appear out of the lift.

It looks like they've had about two hours sleep as well — still elegant and composed but washed out, blinking at the morning light seeping into The Cendryll. Casper's grey suit is matched with a pink shirt and tie, while his sister's red dress makes her look like she's off to a ball.

I wonder if they ever look a mess, slouching around in their pyjamas at night. Something tells me no but it would be funny to see. Humour doesn't seem to be on the agenda this morning, though as Casper rubs his fingers together: a signal for the Quij to collect a book from the shelves located under the skylight.

"Apologies for waking you at this hour," Philomeena says as we reach them. She's holding a red handbag that matches her dress, making me wonder if she's going out for a stroll through Founders' Quad.

"No problem," Conrad says, holding his hand open to welcome a flurry of Quij.

With Casper's book delivered, the small insects glow a fluorescent green and blue, happy to have company in the early hours.

"We thought it important to explain our decision regarding our recent intervention."

"You don't have to explain," I say, knowing they will anyway.

"Of course we do," Casper replies, adjusting the cuffs of his pink shirt.

He's every bit a grand wizard — brooding, elegant and mysterious — the immaculate brown skin marked by scars hidden beneath his suit. He's not as scarred as Farraday but not far off either. The face is unmarked, though, the hands marked showing faint scars: medals of honour for the leader of The Cendryll.

"We sent you on a trip to Zilom, putting you on individual paths of wisdom. The people you met will appear again in due course."

"Why?" Conrad prompts.

"Because as you grow your world will expand," Philomeena replies, taking lipstick out of her handbag. "There's much more to the Society than meets the eye. More than you can experience in a lifetime."

She obviously *is* going out at this crazy hour, dressed like she's got a table booked at Velerin's: the restaurant shaped like a snow-globe in The Winter Quarter.

I know about her secretive relationship with Weyen Lyell, the Caribbean legend in The Orium Circle. Maybe their morning meetings are the only way to get some alone time, similar to the romantic flights Conrad and I take to get away from it all. Philomeena's got business to attend to before she goes though, clicking the lipstick closed as she returns it to her bag.

"There's a chasm in Taeia, creating a potential problem in our world or above ground. Expulsion sounds like the obvious option, but not when you consider how volatile he is. The last war began with Searings above ground: the mark of an evil wizard gathering his army."

"So, you think he's evil?" I ask, watching the Quij complete a ring of light around The Seating Station.

"He has the potential for evil," Casper replies, sitting alongside me, "as we all do. The question we need to consider the most is which option is the least dangerous ... kicking him out or increasing his skill and knowledge? Even with his memory of the S.P.M.A. removed, the buried fury would still be there.

The only way to eradicate that is through rehabilitation, which we can't do, making the decision more difficult. Impulsive decisions rarely improve the problem, leaving it broken into smaller pieces."

"So, you're going to train him?"

"Yes, Guppy, with help," replies Casper, "addressing what I've been avoiding. I spent years trying to distance myself from a father marked with darkness; a father who turned out to be our saviour. If anything, I owe it to my father to train a relative in the art of negotiating darkness."

"And you're going to need us to help?" Conrad prompts, struggling to keep his eyes open.

"No, Conrad. We need you to trust us."

"Of course we trust you."

"It will lead to other rumblings," Philomeena explains, glancing at the row of doors behind The Seating Station — her exit to a morning rendezvous. "You've convinced many of the importance of the Night Rangers; now we've got to remind the cynical few of the necessity for compassion. It's a risk which we're fully aware of and one our reputation rests on."

"Well, Taeia couldn't ask for better teachers," I say, offering the brother and sister duo a smile.

They've stepped back from active duty in the S.P.M.A., knowing when to add their particular touch of magic when needed.

"Who's going to help out?" Conrad asks.

"Jacob," Philomeena replies, spraying herself with a bottle of perfume. "We will teach specific lessons but Jacob will oversee things, making a decision on Taeia's future on his eighteenth birthday — six months from now."

"Transformation or rehabilitation," I comment, understanding the plan.

It's a simple compromise: guide a lost boy back to his senses or alter them forever.

"I bet Jacob can't wait."

"He's a teacher at heart, ready for the challenge," Casper adds, rubbing the back of his neck. "If our gamble pays off, we'll have another teacher in The Cendryll soon."

"So, no more Night Ranging for Taeia."

"Teaching or transformation are the only choices he has left. What we need from the two of you is a heightened alertness. Our decision has already gone down badly with some."

"In The Cendryll?" Conrad asks.

"In our establishments in the above-ground world," Philomeena replies, "where we're headed now."

"*We?*"

"The reason we called you here this morning — to spread the message of patience to the Society gossips, spreading unhelpful rumours."

I want to ask *why us* but decide against it. Asking more questions will only drag things out and if knocking on a few doors gets me back into my bed, I'm all for it. I've got a good idea of the people stirring things up: comrades who prefer idle chatter to more dangerous duties.

I'm sure they'll get the message when we turn up, realising they're now on the watch list for witches and wizards with loose tongues. Not being in the mood for conversation, I'll keep things brief, maybe adding a little explosion as I leave. Well, *someone* needs to pay for dragging me out of bed this early.

———

WE GET OUR INSTRUCTIONS ONCE WE'RE ON FOUNDERS' Quad, the morning air helping to keep me alert. We've each got six places to visit, sharing the message of patience without freaking people out. Society gossips are nervous types masquerading as brave souls, meaning they'll spill their whispers until we've suggested otherwise.

The aim is to share a message of consideration in sensitive times; it should do the trick. Obviously, I don't want to go down the annoying Night Ranger path but I'm in a mischievous mood, mainly because I'm dog tired with minimal patience.

"I'll be asleep when you get back," Conrad says, giving me a comical wink. "Tucked up in bed."

"Don't worry, I'll wake you up," I reply with a smile.

"I might be snoring."

"A choke hold normally does the trick."

"You're such a romantic."

"Don't wait up," I joke, adjusting the black top that completes my ninja look.

They'll be no ninja moves this morning, just a few friendly visits to share the message of trust and tolerance, and then it's back to a warm bed which I don't plan to leave for a while. I've done my fair share of Society duty recently, leaving me to focus on love for a while.

23

QUESTIONABLE APPRENTICE

I hang out in The Cendryll for the next few days, keeping Night Ranging to a minimum. My visits above ground did the trick, persuading members to manage their loose tongues. 'A sensitive issue that won't be improved by rumour: Casper's request.' Rumour spreads quickly in the S.P.M.A., Scribberals rattling to signal another twist to feed theories of favouritism.

I'm still not completely sure what Casper's up to but favouritism probably isn't it. He's spent his life defending the Society, weakened by the last war and worried about Kaira who, rumour has it, is returning for a visit. Everything's a little less magical without Kaira around, probably because it all started with the three of us: Jacob, Kaira and me. Conrad joined a little later, completing the quartet who guided the adults to the heart of a dark mystery.

Maybe Kaira will be able to explain what her dad's *really* up to, deciding to train Taeia with Jacob's help. I also haven't caught up with my brother to ask how he feels about the news, now burdened with training another volatile student.

Conrad's gone above ground to catch up with Noah —

some issue with Lucy that requires a friend's ear. As it's 'girl trouble' as Noah likes to put, I agree to leave the boys to it, imagining them talking through things in their usual way: minimal words leading to a mysterious clarity I can only grasp at.

Lucy hasn't got in touch yet, suggesting it's more serious than Noah thinks. He's always been a bit oblivious in the romantic department; I hope he hasn't messed up badly because he's found someone good in Lucy.

Jacob's appearance cheers me up, a wave from a brother preparing for another day of teaching with a new student to deal with. He looks more alert this morning, shaking hands with Elin Farraday who whispers something in his ear. Jacob nods earnestly, suggesting a continuing conversation as opposed to a new one. Maybe I'm the only one on the outside of this mini mystery, almost certainly to do with Casper's decision to train his nephew.

Logically, he should have kicked Taeia out but he hasn't, offering guilt as an excuse. I get the argument that a problem in the Society is a problem above ground. Yes, we can remove memories of all things magical but unless rehabilitation takes place, hidden venom remains. So, the theory goes that Taeia needs to be offered a second chance of redemption, following my attempt on The Hallowed Lawn.

I can't think of anyone else who's had a second chance so, on the surface, it looks like the rumoured favouritism buzzing in Scribberals. There's a lot more to Casper Renn than meets the eye, though, and nothing's done without the benefit of our magical world in mind. Taeia's a problem, all right, but maybe not for the reasons Casper's suggesting.

I just hope Kaira gets here soon so we can catch up on lost time, discussing our adventures and her dad's involvement in a new mystery. A tap on the shoulder from Jacob helps me refocus on the job at hand, finding out more about his role in the training of a questionable apprentice.

"I guess you've heard," he says, sipping Liqin from a steel cup.

It looks like he's still struggling with headaches or a lack of sleep. At least he seems less burdened which can only be a good thing.

"Yep," I say, brushing my brown hair behind my ears.

Jacob sits alongside me in Quandary Corner, the small bay tucked away behind The Seating Station. It's where I spent my early days in The Cendryll when I was the only underage member here. I was generally ignored then until Kaira turned up and the fun started. Something tells me the adventures are about to start again.

"The sort of problem I've been trying to avoid," Jacob adds, adjusting the Society tie he hates wearing.

I glance at the silver bracelet on his right wrist — his birthday present from me with the tiny photograph of mum and the both of us. It's no coincidence that Casper has asked Jacob to take Taeia under his wing. After all, it was Casper and Philomeena who gave our mum a second chance, so it makes sense for the burden to fall on us this time.

"I'll be around to help and Kaira's on her way back, apparently."

"I doubt she'll stay long."

"What makes you say that?"

"The Renns don't do random," Jacob explains, sipping his Liqin as the doors swing open and closed — the flurry of witches and wizards going about their business. "Kaira's coming back for a reason, just like I've been asked to train this idiot Night Ranger for a reason."

"I agree," I reply, taking the steel cup from Jacob. I've got my own headache to deal with, including a new puzzle concerning Kaira's return. "So, what were you and Elin whispering about?"

"Plans for Taeia."

"Which are?"

"Speeding up the process to find out what he's made of."

"What's the hurry?"

"That's the part I don't know but Casper asking me to train Taeia, Elin whispering in my ear and Kaira returning: I think it's fair to say they're all linked."

"How?"

"You tell me, Nancy Drew," he replies with a smile. "We'll find out more when Kaira gets here."

"I wonder where she's been ... beyond the places we've travelled to, I mean."

"Far and wide, according to Elin."

"Really? Like where?"

"Places I've never heard of and don't know how to get to."

I take another sip of Jacob's yellow remedy, a familiar sensation running through me. The idea of an infinite, expanding universe has hovered over us from the early days, but I decided to stay with Jacob, waving Kaira off on her travels.

"So, you think Kaira's return links to Taeia?" I ask, holding Jacob's gaze.

He takes the silver cup back, nodding as he sips the Liqin. "Yep, which probably means trouble for us."

"In what way?"

"When was the last time we said no to Kaira? Even when that meant walking onto a battlefield?"

"We all made our own choices, Jacob."

"Of course, but if Kaira's coming back for more than a

visit, it means she's seen things ... things she needs to tell us about."

"Bad things, you mean?"

"Or things she doesn't like the look of."

"Maybe she's just missed us. You've got a habit of over-thinking things, big brother."

"And you've got a sense of things. Why do you think Kaira's coming back?"

Looking up at the skylight lending its soft glow to the morning activity, I remember the first time we walked beneath it — a spacewalk leading to Conrad and his dad, hiding out in the secret space for members under suspicion.

I knew then that Theodore was involved in whatever was brewing in the S.P.M.A. Luckily, it turned out his only crime was a loose tongue: a mistake he more than made up for. Although I don't know why Kaira's returning, Jacob's right: the Renns *don't* do random so it looks like I'll be venturing to new places before too long.

———

WITH JACOB HEADING OFF FOR ANOTHER DAY OF TEACHING, I take the lift to the fourth floor. I wait for the intense group of wizards to cross The Floating Floor, stepping back to avoid the swinging arms of the thinnest of the group, lowering his voice as he spots me.

"Miss Grayling," he offers with a forced smile as if I'm marked with a strange curse that might infect him.

It's obvious that our visits above ground this morning haven't stopped the rumours: people are annoyed at Casper's choice to train an errant Night Ranger. I just hope I find out what the bigger issue is soon because energy only

changes in a magical faculty due to fear, fury or concern —
and it's changing now.

Judging from the forced smile I just got, things are at the
'concern' level, but it won't take long for the doubts to creep
in. It's time for me to park thoughts of Night Ranging and
plot a way through this new puzzle. I close the door to my
fourth-floor quarters, studying the rooms that once
belonged to Kaira's aunt, Philomeena.

Being sixteen affords you certain levels of privacy,
meaning I won't be bothered unless Conrad returns, but
once Noah gets talking he's hard to stop. I've got enough
time to study the map on my bedroom ceiling, reflecting on
all the places I've been to or heard of. It's a starting point in
the search for a new unknown: the real reason a fallen Night
Ranger's been given another chance.

Churchill, Kaira's cat, is perched on the windowsill of
the bedroom, looking a little unimpressed with the state of
the room. I can tidy up later but now's the time for questions, helped by the map I reveal with the utterance of
'Exhibius' ... an intricate illustration appearing in the centre
of the ceiling ... the surrounding space ready to be filled in
as I uncover the expanding universe I call home.

The Shallows, Drandok and The Royisin Heights have
been added recently, moving images offering an impression
of the character of each realm. Silverbacks rise in the air,
struggling in the taming range meant to mute their fury. The
tiny figures roaming in the taming range are likely to be
Orgev's group, triggering the first question. Are the taming
of the Silverbacks linked to this strange turn of events?

Secondly, was our meeting in Zilom linked to a bigger
question surrounding Taeia Renn? Looking back, it was an
elaborate way for the Society elders to share their concerns

regarding a rogue comrade: a note in a Scribberal would have done the job.

The pieces start falling into place. The appearance of Aarav Khan, standing on a pathway of light that stretched into the sky; Casper sending help when we tracked down Taeia in the trading lane of Tallis & Crake; the public duel between Taeia and the white Williynx he harmed: one elaborate maze of movements for a teenage boy with a bad temper.

As the moving map of magic flickers on the ceiling, one thing becomes obvious ... the training of a fallen Night Ranger is masking something else ... something bigger that links to Kaira's return.

"Undilum," I utter, watching the map fade away as I lie down on my bed, patting for Churchill to join me.

With Kaira's cat at the foot of the bed, I wonder what my best friend's seen on her travels and how it links to a decision that's drawing us back together.

24

A WAITING GAME

I leave the Night Ranging to Conrad and Noah, deciding to stay put in The Cendryll, counting down the hours before Kaira's return. Lucy's also taking a night off from Society duty which suggests Noah's messed up in some way, leaving Conrad to lend a friendly ear.

Noah can talk for England so they'll probably end up in Rebel's Rest for a few hours, Noah sinking Jysyn Juice like it's going out of fashion, ruminating on the complications of love. Conrad and Noah can discuss the mysteries of girls, and I can wait for Kaira to walk through one of the doors lining the ground floor.

No one's said anything about Kaira returning tonight, but the look on her dad and aunt's face says it all. They're unusually animated, moving along the five floors of The Cendryll, having in-depth conversations with various members.

Elin Farraday is the person Casper and Philomeena talk to the most before he returns to his third-floor quarters, battling with the multi-coloured powders and various remedies, trying to unlock the secret to a new charm. His brother, the Farraday I know best, appears from the lift as evening falls and members exit through the swinging doors, turning in for the night.

The night has just begun for me so I perch in Quandary Corner, feeling a rush of reminiscence as I study the door Kaira first walked through: a black door that doesn't fit its frame properly, almost hanging off the hinges as it sweeps witches and wizards to their desired destinations. Kaira's chosen to stay away for two years, meeting her dad and aunt in the places she's journeyed to, never once passing through Society Square to say hello.

I must admit I was a little hurt at first, also understanding my friend needed space from a magical universe that's taken so much from her family. Society duty suits me but battle has marked us all in different ways, although I always hoped the four of us would be drawn together again.

Jacob's got his teaching duties and Night Ranging takes up mine and Conrad's time, which brings me back to the puzzle surrounding Kaira's return. The fact Casper and Philomeena haven't fully explained things suggests there's a new web forming. I just hope it's not another web of secrets to unravel, largely because one of the biggest lessons the adults learnt was the limitations of secrecy — blinding rather than illuminating.

The remaining Quij hover high above, circling below The Cendryll's skylight in a pre-sleep ritual. Soon, I'll be sitting in darkness with Farraday and the Society stragglers for company: the name for the handful of comrades who roam the landings, using Periums to find company when the evenings get lonely.

Quandary Corner is my thinking spot, adding a touch of privacy ideal for an evening of reflection. I could activate a Spintz charm but decide against it, preferring the solitude of darkness. Jacob's encouraged me to manage my expectations regarding Kaira, something he mentioned after another long day of teaching.

"A lot can change in two years," he advised, finding me holed up in my bedroom. "Just don't expect Kaira to be the same or want the same things you do."

"Meaning what?"

"Meaning things won't necessarily go back to how they were."

I remember my brother's words as I glance down at a blank pamphlet on the floor. All members have a habit of doing this, checking to make sure the Society pamphlet — *No News is Good News* — stays blank. No news means no trouble, something we're all keen to maintain.

The Society elders have done a lot to maintain peace, including creature taming, the healing cells of Drandok and a training regime for an underage wizard who's causing concern. Managing malice is the name of the game, resolving problems before they morph into bigger ones. It's better than ignoring the darkness that's buried in all of us — a fine balancing act requiring constant surveillance and intervention.

A circle of fire gets my attention, Farraday's way of signalling his approach. He uses his fingers to spin another three circles into action, adding more until I stop dwelling on 'What ifs' and allow a smile to form.

"Hey," I say, watching Farraday guide the circles of fire above Quandary Corner.

"What's The Fire Witch brooding on?" he asks, adding links between the circles.

"I'm sure you know."

"Kaira?"

I nod, laughing as the connected circles of fire spin

around my body: a simple charm to draw me out of my introspection. "Do you know why she's coming back?"

"She's missed us all."

"*Farraday.*"

"Okay. She's missed us all and has a few stories to tell."

He brushes the thinning hair over his face, a habit he uses to hide his scars. The familiar uniform of black trousers, black leather jacket and brown waistcoat remains — a wizarding legend with a knack of appearing whenever he's needed.

"She could have used a Scribberal to send her stories."

"They're too *juicy* for a Scribberal," Farraday adds with a mischievous look, deciding to add fire moths to the circles surrounding me.

"Trouble in wonderland?" I ask.

"Don't get any ideas."

"I could do with a bit of trouble, to be honest. A few days of dodging death to keep me sharp."

Farraday laughs at this, drawing the appearance of a nervous witch at the top of the spiral staircase. "It's only me, Juna, keeping Guppy company."

"With fire?" the jumpy witch asks, gripping onto her nightgown that's seen better days.

"I was thinking of a sandwich but she didn't look hungry. She's having an emotional blip."

I give Farraday a look, wishing he had produced a sandwich because I'm *starving*.

"Well, sleep might help her emotional state. Even Night Rangers need to rest."

"Agreed, general," Farraday replies, saluting comically before he sends a circle of fire towards the wandering witch who decides to call it a night.

"What's with the fire?" I ask as we head over to the

empty Seating Station, the skylight offering minimal illumination tonight.

"Keeping you warm for the grand arrival."

"Any idea what time that might be?"

"You can't rush genius," Farraday jokes.

"You're really not helping."

"Kaira will be here soon, Guppy. Relax and wait for your penchant to vibrate."

I study my silver bracelet, rubbing the topaz-blue gemstones to feel their warmth. "What do you think about Taeia being trained instead of being kicked out?" I decide to ask.

"Casper works in mysterious ways."

"Tell me about it."

"But his mystery always includes logic. Keeping Taeia close for now is more beneficial, although we'll see how that plays out in the long run."

"Do you think he's got darkness in him?"

"Who hasn't?"

"You know what I mean, Farraday."

"I think he struggles with it more than most — the reason kicking him out and removing his memory won't solve the problem. Darkness above-ground still needs to be managed; we rely on the non-magical world, after all."

"Kaira's return must be linked to Taeia and the others: Odin, Neve and probably Alice Aradel's appearance in The Shallows."

"Maybe," Farraday replies, transforming the rings of fire into daisy chains of light.

"*Definitely*," I counter, adding my own decoration to the daisy chain. "She's learnt things on her travels that link to things going on here. It's why some of The Cendryll members look concerned; I just can't link it all together."

"Well, if you're right, that's what Kaira's coming back to help with."

"Before she heads off again."

"Depends on where she is in her journey," Farraday comments. "Everyone comes home in the end, Guppy, even those who want to forget the things that haunt them."

"She watched her granddad die," I say, recalling the final sacrifice of seven in The Saralin Sands. "I doubt she'll ever get over that."

"And Conrad watched his father suffer the same fate. It's not a matter of getting over death but learning to live with it. Travel helps to distract, but that's all. This return will be the first of many — the start of Kaira's realisation that what's missing is what she's left behind. Until then, hold onto the time you have with her."

I hope Farraday's right and the bond is still strong, but things have changed in the two years since Kaira's been gone: new loves, fading forces and fallen comrades. I sit with Farraday in the evening light of The Cendryll, hoping Kaira will appear in the daisy chain of light soon: the friend who started an adventure of a lifetime.

IT'S PAST MIDNIGHT WHEN FARRADAY LEAVES, NUDGING ME awake to say farewell. He's completed his journey in the military sense, no longer tied to duty in the way he was. That's fallen on younger soldiers now, myself included.

"You can always go to bed; I'm sure Kaira knows the way."

I mumble goodnight, curled up on the outer circle of The Seating Station, needing to welcome Kaira back if she does arrive. It's weird that her dad and aunt haven't appeared, raising doubts about the timing of her return, but something keeps me on the ground floor of The Cendryll: a need to know where I am with my old friend.

Things move on and people leave you, I guess, but that's never stopped me wishing that the four of us would reform one day — Jacob and Kaira tempted back to the wizarding adventures that form some of my best memories. The blaze of light that appears in the daisy chain isn't what I hope for ... Kaira's dad and aunt appearing to keep me company.

Philomeena reaches up to a section of the glimmering daisy chain, kneeling to decorate the floor with a similar pattern: a carpet of welcome for an invisible guest. As brother and sister walk through the tunnel of light, I struggle to keep my eyes open.

"Kaira said you'd wait up," Philomeena says, offering me a vial of Fillywiss as she sits alongside me.

I gulp it down, not feeling lightheaded but happy for anything to keep me awake.

"I can't believe it's been two years."

"Two years of worry," Casper comments.

"You miss her a lot, I can tell"

"Of course, Guppy, but I was forced to let go far earlier than anticipated. Kaira follows her aunt's footsteps in the ways of healing: distance and time."

"So, she's coming back because she's slowly healing?"

"Or perhaps she can't," Philomeena replies, "realising scars form whichever world you travel to."

I study the daisy chain of light, thinking about the scars marking my own body that I avoid looking at ... a sense they will always be the bond that binds us together ... a young quartet who fought to the death to keep a magical world alive.

25

A WANDERER'S RETURN

I wake up to find a familiar face sitting on the bed next to me: a friend who's finally returned to the place we first met.

"Kaira!" I shout, leaping out of bed to give her the biggest hug I can muster.

"Hello, stranger," she replies with a laugh I've missed so much.

She's a little taller, dressed in jeans and a more formal upper half: white shirt and blue coat. Nothing much else has changed, though — the black hair and caramel skin reminding me of the girl I first met in the very faculty we're in now. I feel the same bond within seconds of seeing my best friend: the girl destined to fight for a magical Society's survival.

"When did you get here?"

"About an hour after you fell asleep. Thanks for the pathway of light, by the way — very romantic."

We find our old rhythm straight away, laughing as I tell her about my life as a Night Ranger and Conrad, of course. She doesn't seem as keen to share stories of her travels, explaining that Jacob and Conrad are in the dining room, waiting for us.

This confirms what I originally thought ... that whatever Casper's up to is linked to Kaira's return ... so the only thing left to do is get showered and dressed, hoping the friend I've missed is going to stay for a while.

I know Kaira hasn't come back for good, something about her need to maintain a distance from past events. It doesn't mean she's left the S.P.M.A. behind though ... she's just moving in her own direction towards other magical spaces, providing her with whatever she's looking for.

The conversation will turn to our individual adventures soon enough, but first we need to relearn each other's rhythms before we get to the 'juicy' stuff, as Farraday puts it.

"I've got a lot to tell you," Kaira says with a familiar smile.

She doesn't offer more and I don't ask, realising her return is linked to the four of us: Kaira, Jacob, Conrad and me — the old army regrouping for unknown reasons. It doesn't take a genius to work out it's probably linked to the mess Taeia's made, along with Casper's offer to train him with Jacob's help. Everything is done for a reason in the S.P.M.A., including the return of a loyal friend.

"It's good to see you, Kaira," I say, grabbing a towel from my wardrobe. "I've missed you."

"I've missed you more," she quips before adding, "an interesting selection of clothes."

She nods towards the row of grey, white and black T-shirts hung up in the wardrobe: Conrad's collection I like to keep near. "How's boy wonder?"

"Sexy," I reply, making us laugh again.

I don't get any updates on Kaira's love life but I know she'll tell me in time. Two years is plenty of time for romance even when you're on the move. She looks more like her aunt now — the ever-elegant Philomeena Renn who keeps an eye on things with her brother.

Her silver penchant bracelet is one of the many things we share, except for the different coloured gemstones. We also share a history of isolation in our first days in The Cendryll: two lost girls trying to navigate the beauty and mystery we'd been plunged into. We also share the scars of war, including the echo of loss reverberating with thoughts of fallen soldiers.

We're in a different phase now, the Society at peace except for mild rumblings which are being dealt with. As I step into the bathroom, buzzing with excitement, I wonder where Kaira's going to lead us. Wherever it leads, I'm ready to go but first I need to get ready before a new whirlwind of information forms.

I FIND KAIRA, JACOB AND CONRAD SITTING AT THE DINING room table. Toast is piled on plates with silver tea cups on a tray. The three of them are chatting away, laughing at the memory of the good old days when we were all together. We're not headed for another war, hopefully, but there's a list of questions running through my head — questions Kaira can answer hopefully.

"Come on, Guppy," Jacob encourages as he puts another plate of toast on the table. "Your best friend's back and you're dawdling."

I sit alongside Kaira, happy to be alongside my friend again. It's the feeling I've missed ... the sense of family I get when I'm around the three people who mean the most. I've always felt invincible around them and I get the same feeling now as I bite into a piece of toast.

"So, Kaira, spill the beans," Conrad states as he sips his tea, no magical remedy required this morning.

"Give her time to eat," Jacob adds, reverting to his role of guardian of the young.

We don't need his protection now, of course, but it still feels good to fall back into old rhythms.

"It's good to see you all," Kaira comments as she sips her tea, glancing at the rickety doors in the rooms once occupied by her aunt.

We shared my bedroom for a long time, growing up around the mystery and mayhem swirling in the Society. I've kept the drawings of charms, artefacts and creatures on the walls as a memory of our time together, hoping this moment would arrive when we had a chance to reconnect on new adventures.

"Are you staying long?" I ask, reaching for another piece of a toast.

"Long enough to have some fun," Kaira replies with a mischievous smile, her flawless skin giving a glimpse of the beauty she's going to be.

She's got stories, all right, but is playing the cool card at the moment, something Renns are known for.

"I suppose you've heard about the rumblings here," Jacob adds, pouring more tea for us all.

Kaira nods, running her fingers over the surface of the dining table. "A few people losing their balance."

"More like losing their heads," Conrad counters, gesturing for me to pass the jam.

"You're taller," Kaira says in reply to Conrad's question, "and it looks like Jacob's shrunk a bit."

"All those kids driving me mad," Jacob jokes, getting a

laugh from us all, but the 'balance' comment has got our attention.

It's the first clue that Kaira's return is what I suspected … linked to the characters we've been tracking recently.

"So, what do you think it means?" I prompt, my old impatience returning. "The lack of balance we're seeing in some?"

Kaira turns to me before adding, "Now, *that's* the question I've been waiting for."

"So, you *do* know?" Conrad asks.

"Of course she knows," I reply. "That's why Kaira's back … to fill us in on the new rumblings."

"How's Farraday?" Kaira asks as a flicker of sadness crosses her face, probably linked to the death of Farraday's closest comrade — Smyck — the man who gave his life to save hers.

"He's getting about," Jacob replies, deciding to take the Society tie off, enjoying the few hours before teaching starts again. "The Royisin Heights is his favourite haunt at the moment. Well, the underground section mainly; the remedies help with his scars."

"Sianna's hideout as well," Kaira adds, causing me to glance at the others.

It's like she's been keeping an eye on us since she's been away — something that shouldn't come as a surprise — but it's connected to something bigger: I *know* it is.

"Sianna's chosen to step back from Society duty," I say. "You know, after watching her granddad locked into an obsessive guard over the thing that almost destroyed us."

"It would have been enough to put anyone off for life," Conrad adds, hanging his grey coat over the back of the chair. "Francis had no life in the end, the reason he warned us off committing to the Society."

"But here we all are," Kaira replies, lifting her teacup in a strange salute. "Society soldiers to the core."

"I thought you'd left it all behind?"

"No, Conrad, just another way of living in our weird and wonderful world."

"So, why have you come back?"

"To show you that world."

"*What*?" Conrad and I say in unison, leaving only Jacob to stay silent.

My brother knows more than he's letting on, but all will be revealed soon enough so I let things unravel, sipping my tea as questions flood my mind. *Another world*? What the hell does that mean?

"If you clear the table, I can show you," Kaira states, standing to take off her coat.

With Jacob and Conrad left to clear the table, she leans over to give me a hug, whispering, "You're going to love this."

The only words I need to hear to ignite the fire ... my heart pounding at the thought of another magical adventure.

26

HEIR TO THE SKIES

With the table cleared and questions on the tip of my tongue, Kaira activates the Canvia charm — a creative charm allowing the user to generate any image required. It's her way of showing us the world she's referred to: a world beyond our knowledge that must be linked to the S.P.M.A. in some way, but how?

Instead of dealing with our endless questions, Kaira decides to show us, generating a triangle of light that hovers above the dining table, only adding to the mystery.

"We might need something stronger than tea for this part," she suggests with a smile, revelling in what she's about to reveal.

I've got no idea what the purple triangle of light means, racking my brains to remember a faculty or realm shaped like this, but I can't think of one. So, it must be elsewhere ... beyond The Society Sphere in places I haven't ventured or been instructed to visit.

Dangerous realms, maybe, with their own magic and malevs, maintaining a delicate balance of peace and compromise. Either way, I'm already fizzing with excitement at the thought of travelling there.

With a Parasil placed on the dining table, we fill our cups with Jysyn Juice before Kaira begins. She's mentioned that her dad and aunt have decided to leave us to it, recognising we need time to reconnect and digest Kaira's revelations — revelations I can't wait to hear.

As the purple triangle of light hovering above the table, I sip my Jysyn Juice, steadying the tremor in my hand as the adrenaline kicks in.

"Firstly, I just want to say how much I've missed you all; a feeling that grew stronger the longer I stayed away. Certain things kept me away longer than I expected ... things I'm going to show you now."

"We've missed you too, Kaira," Jacob adds. "It hasn't been the same without you."

"Second that," Conrad says. "Guppy talks about you all the time; it was weird not having you around."

"Well, I'm back now — for a while at least — and I'll be back for good soon, assuming we can sort things out *here*."

With this, Kaira points to the triangle of light, touching the edges to spin it above the dining table. As it spins, sections form within the triangle ... dots filling the sections as they do on a Tabulal: another surveillance device used by The Orium Circle. Tabulals identify war lines which makes me wonder if this is what we're looking at now: a thread Kaira picks up on.

"The dots will form into words when we touch them."

"Names of the different realms?" Jacob guesses, getting a nod from Kaira.

"Where's this 'new world' you're talking about?" Conrad asks.

"In the sky," Kaira replies, spinning the triangle again to

activate more sections within the triangle. "It's known as the sky realms, accessible by winged creatures who can travel through sky portals."

"Williynx and sky urchins," I add, gulping down my Jysyn Juice and reaching for the tap on the Parasil.

The glass container refills itself, the green liquid bubbling as it rises within the Parasil: magic, of course.

With my silver teacup refilled, Kaira continues, blowing on the edges of the triangle, transforming it into a 3D image. This allows us to get a greater sense of the realms forming ... floating palaces in one and wild oceans in another. The one that draws my attention the most is the realm nearest to me, figures hovering in packs before they swarm down on dead creatures.

The place is *wild* and full of the high octane drama I've been missing, not that I'm looking for another war but *magical adventure* is what the S.P.M.A. is all about to me, meaning new places and new characters — some more friendly than others.

"So, you've been there?" Conrad asks. "To the sky realms?"

"Yep," Kaira replies, touching the dots in a corner section of the floating triangle. "Not all this time. I stayed in Senreiya for a while, enjoying the peace and tranquillity of the place. I found out about the sky realms in Senreiya, partly because it's one of the highest realms in The Society Sphere."

"Close to The Devenant in the sky," I add.

"So, The Devenant is how you access the sky realms?" Jacob asks as he studies the floating triangle of light. "Without a winged creature, I mean."

"Not quite," Kaira adds, touching the dots in one of the realms until an image of connected pathways appear, leading to a sprawling mass of white that dominates the landscape. "Apart from getting there on the back of winged creatures, the sky realms are accessed via channels that can be opened by whoever controls each realm."

"And who controls this one?" Conrad asks, pointing to the white mound of concrete surrounded by a hundred pathways.

"The Winter King."

"Someone you've met?"

"No."

"But he's linked to why you've come back," I prompt, sensing our journey's going to start sooner than I anticipated.

"Yes, Guppy," Kaira replies. "In a nutshell, the sky realms are a fragile triangle of allegiances, similar to where the S.P.M.A. was two years."

"And it's all part of the same universe?" Jacob asks, struggling to make the connection between a Winter King and the known realms within and beyond the Society.

"All part of the same connected universe, yes, but like the realms beyond the Society Sphere, each has its own laws and tensions — fragile allegiances fraying as The Winter King weakens."

"But if you haven't met him, how does he link to what's going on with us and the S.P.M.A.?" I ask, wondering why Kaira's taking such an elaborate route around this.

"Because The Winter King is a Renn and his heir is causing problems in our world."

"*Taeia*?" I utter, putting the silver teacup down as the tremor in my hand worsens. "You've *got* to be kidding me?"

"I wish I was, Guppy but as you know, fate has a way of calling the Renns and there's no way off the path you're set on. If there was, I wouldn't have ended up in a fire fight with an evil wizard two years ago."

"So, we've got another fight on our hands?" Jacob states, reaching for the last piece of toast.

"Maybe," Kaira replies, brushing her hair behind her ears. "That all depends on Taeia and how his training goes."

"The reason your dad hasn't kicked him out," Conrad adds, refilling his silver teacup with the remedy for bravery.

"Right, because kicking him out just sends a potential psychopath above ground. My dad thought bringing Taeia into the Society with limited training might work, knowing he couldn't leave him to descend into a darkness that's roaring to get out."

"The reason he's been firing out at witches and wizards, including us," I add.

"Right," Kaira replies, "so now we have something else to tame along with the Silverbacks."

"I still don't get the point of taming them," Conrad comments.

"They can fly," I reply, beginning to get how it's all connected. "It's another way of testing the Domitus' loyalty. One, we give them a mild curse to tame the Silverbacks with, causing no lasting damage. Two, we allow them to fly the tamed creatures, seeing how many of them try to seek passage to the sky realms — another way of uncovering malevs in our midst."

"As sharp as ever, Guppy," Kaira offers with a smile: a smile I've missed from a friend with an ability to unify people.

"The reason Taeia was given Night Ranger status," Jacob adds, "testing how soon he'd look for the sky realms on discovering they existed."

"Yes, Jacob," Kaira adds, studying the white, concrete

structure surrounding by one hundred pathways: war lines or walkways to allies in neighbouring realms. It looks like we're going to find out soon enough.

"And when Taeia finds out he's heir to The Winter King?" Conrad prompts.

"We make a decision on what we do," Kaira replies. "The sky realms are a connected universe, but separate in other ways."

"Meaning?"

"Meaning it has its own protective shell: not The Devenant but something else."

"So, if it's under threat we're not?" I ask.

"That's right, although once Taeia gets wind of his destiny, he's likely to cause havoc in the sky and on the ground below."

"So, we stop him before that happens," Jacob comments, standing from his chair as the clock in the dining room strikes eight a.m.

"No pressure then, big brother," I joke. "Just a matter of training an unhinged boy out of his bad habits."

"Luckily, he's not a man yet," Jacob replies, picking up the Society tie from the table and tying it as loosely as possible. "We've got six months before his eighteenth birthday ... when we can convert him into a Melackin if need be."

"It could be a long six months," Kaira adds, spinning the triangle once more as the realms surrounding The Winter King's fortress glitter into view. "Until then, we've all got a job to do. I need to build the trust of Thylas Renn: the name of The Winter King."

"So, is he your great grandfather?" Conrad asks.

"My great-great-great ... I could go on but I don't really know," Kaira adds with another smile, bringing a moment of laughter to an impending drama. "He's survived for so long on the blood of the dead."

"Vampires and madmen in the family, then," Jacob quips, bringing more laughter.

"No vampires as far as I know," Kaira replies, studying the purple triangle of light spinning slowly above the table. "It's a way of extending life, similar to how we use the Laudlum remedy in the S.P.M.A."

"Just a bit more gross," I say, not as keen to finish my Jysyn Juice with thoughts of drinking blood running through my mind.

"Then there's the Bloodseekers who also live off the blood of the dead; they're not as friendly."

"You're joking?" Conrad says, almost spitting out his mouthful of Jysyn Juice.

"The figures you see swarming over dead creatures here," Kaira adds, pointing to the groups I saw form earlier.

"So, Bloodseekers; a Winter King who drinks blood to stay strong and an ex Night Ranger who's turning into a nutter, soon to be crowned the next Winter King. Where do we sign up?"

"I bet you're glad I'm back," Kaira jokes as she stands, rolling up the sleeves on her white shirt.

"So, what happens next?" Jacob asks, ready to head off for another day of teaching.

"You keep an eye on Taeia in your lessons and I'll travel with Guppy and Conrad to The Goronoff Mountains: the third contact point between us and the sky realms. The Royisin Heights, Zilom and The Goronoff Mountains make up the triangle of fragile allegiance in the sky. Once you know where to search, you can see the outline of the sky realms in the stars, something I can show you later."

"So, the meeting in Zilom wasn't a coincidence?" I say, putting down my silver teacup.

"Nope," Kaira replies, "and neither was Sianna's appearance in The Royisin Heights. She might be a recluse but she's still a soldier: a sky soldier now like Aarav Khan in Zilom. They watch the skies to keep an eye on who's attempting travel to the sky realms. It's another way of capturing enemies when they scatter, although some slip through with help."

"And I thought you were just soaking up the sun in Gilweean and Senreiya," I comment as I stand, studying my best friend as she deactivates the purple triangle: an extension of our magical world hidden in the sky.

"When do we travel to The Goronoff Mountains?" Conrad asks, "and what do we tell Lucy and Noah who're going to wonder what we're up to?"

"We'll travel there later today. Lucy and Noah can be told at a later date, leaving the decision in their hands."

"Travel with us to the sky realms, you mean?"

"If that's what they choose to do," Kaira replies, "but they'll need more advanced training before that can happen. Night Ranging isn't the same as full combat: an eventuality we have to prepare for."

"You remind me of your dad and aunt more and more," Jacob says, opening the door to return to the buzz of The Cendryll. "A Renn on a mission to heal."

"Let's just hope we can," Kaira adds, offering a wave to Jacob as he leaves: a warrior girl who's returned with news of a fading King in the skies and a lost boy in our circle with malice in his bones.

27

FAMILIAR TONES

The Goronoff Mountains stand like a winged creature, perched to the west of Zilom. The third part of the triangle of fragile allegiance, it looks more like a fortress than a beacon of protection. We made our way out of The Cendryll as daylight faded, Conrad explaining to Lucy and Noah we were spending time with Kaira before she headed off on her travels again.

Like Kaira said, Lucy and Noah will be told about the sky realms soon enough but, for now, I need to understand more about the alignment of the stars, holding the secrets of magical travel to new realms.

Kaira rides the white Williynx once attached to Taeia, the surprising heir to a throne he's currently got no idea about. Let's hope it stays that way until we've mapped the universe hidden in the stars, because if anyone's going to cause us a headache it's Taeia.

He's always had bad energy but so have other witches and wizards. Sometimes, it's just arrogance or emotional distance but in Taeia's case it's deeper: a desire to prove himself in destructive ways. Firing out charms at his comrades is only the start it seems, fated for the dark path Aarav Khan predicted in Zilom.

It's all coming together now: Sianna Follygrin's helping hand in The Royisin Heights; our over-engineered trip to Zilom; Taeia's buried fury and Kaira's return. The Renns are at the heart of things again as they're always likely to be. There's something *royal* about them even in the way Kaira's pointing to the sky now: regal and blessed with unique magical powers.

The two Renns in question are under very different pressures: Taeia under the watchful eye of Kaira's dad, and Thylas Renn under siege as his powers fade: a Winter King calling for help from relatives destined for epic adventures.

The Graylings didn't really do epic until Jacob and I got caught up in the last whirlwind swarming the S.P.M.A. I'm a bit of a whirlwind myself, choosing adventure whenever it presents itself, and I've got the feeling the adventure ahead has *epic* written all over it.

"From where we're standing, The Royisin Heights rests in the north-east with Zilom situated in the lower-east section," Kaira explains. "The Goronoff Mountains occupy the west plain, forming the triangle I showed you in The Cendryll."

"The fragile triangle of allegiance" Conrad adds as Erivan rubs beaks with Oweyna: our feathered friends transporting us through familiar territory.

I remember Oweyna's fury on The Hallowed Lawn, arching over a terrified Taeia who'd punched the rare Williynx out of frustration. No human ever harms any Society creature, making Taeia's second chance on The Hallowed Lawn seem odd at the time.

That was until Kaira turned up, explaining things with a simple triangle of light: another universe in the sky formed of a familiar mixture of magic and malice. There's no evidence of a triangle in the stars so I focus harder on the part of the sky Kaira's pointing to, hoping to see something revealing soon.

"How does it work?" I ask. "Accessing sky realms without winged creatures?"

"Shooting stars and twisted light," Kaira replies, pointing to a falling star descending from the east. "Shooting stars draw little attention in a world where anything's possible, but with the right vision you see *a lot* more."

"With a Quivven?"

"Something simpler," Kaira replies with a smile. "Crilliun."

"Eye drops for night vision."

"Yep."

"Then let's do it," Conrad suggests, reaching for a vial of clear liquid.

"There's something else, though," Kaira adds. "A chasm to view the sky realms through, making sure you're in the right position. The holes marking The Goronoff Mountains are aligned to certain star formations. When the chasm opens, you fall below as the shower of stars and twisted light beam down. It's the same split-second timing needed in battle."

"And then you're transported into the skies?" Conrad asks.

"That's right."

"And we can't just fly through on our Williynx?"

"We can," Kaira adds, "but entering a sky realm without clear passage can go *very wrong*."

"Clear passage?" I query.

"Permission, Guppy. A bit like how things work in Gilweean and Sad Souls. Certain realms aren't accessible to all, meaning procedure has to be followed. The rules are similar to those we followed when we went beyond The Society Sphere.

Our penchants lose their powers because we're entering connected realms. Each realm has its own laws, including the rules of safe passage. Some places can be accessed without a problem, but the sky realms are different."

"In what way?" Conrad prompts.

"Only a few realms in the sky are solid allies of the S.P.M.A. We haven't got enemies, necessarily, but nor do we have strong bonds like we have with the sky urchins."

"So, we need to tread carefully," I add, remembering Yoran's phrase — the wise sky urchin now based in The Cendryll — slow travel and subtle movements.

Something tells me Yoran's part of this growing drama along with Kerevenn. The S.P.M.A. does things *at scale,* including the way it manages tensions, solving problems by mapping everything in micro detail. The details are what we're here to learn, waiting for a chasm to form in The Goronoff Mountains before a spiral of light celebrates our arrival ... light chasing a shower of stars as they fall.

As a flood of adrenaline rushes through me, Kaira rubs Oweyna's neck, causing the Williynx's feathers to stand to attention. It's clear our feathered friend isn't over Taeia's attack, baulking at Kaira's touch initially until her head lowers, releasing a single feather. The feather sends a wisp of light running towards the holes marking the mountains ... light that drips through each gap like light rainfall.

Moments later, the mountains split apart ... a deafening crack thudding in my ear drums as our Williynx squawk. It's a command for us to climb on but Kaira raises a hand, gesturing for us to stay put.

"Stay on your side of the chasm," she explains,

remaining calm as the gap widens between us ... Conrad and I standing one side with Kaira on the other ... three magicians balanced on a colossal bulk of stone shuddering into life.

"What now?" Conrad asks, holding out his arms to keep his balance.

"We wait for the stars to fall followed by a twist of light," Kaira explains, keeping her eyes on the sky.

"Then we jump to our deaths?" I joke.

"You've always loved new adventures," Kaira adds with another smile.

"It feels like we're starting a new one."

"We are."

"When are we going to jump?" Conrad prompts. "Hopefully, before the mountains explode, sending us flying."

"Patience, Conrad," Kaira replies, turning her palms face up, just as Jacob does when he calls the Quij.

A silent streak of green light appears seconds later, twisting through the sky before it descends, looking like a ribbon stretching out towards us. The expected shooting stars appear soon after, falling in a fountain of light until they reach the chasm between us, illuminating the darkness below.

"Who's that?" I ask, pointing the to figure dressed in green *way* down in the mountain chasm.

"Sylvian Creswell," Kaira explains, raising a hand of allegiance. "The sky soldier leading operations in The Goronoff Mountains."

Conrad grabs my hand as I lose my balance, caught off guard as The Goronoff Mountains shudder again. Kaira stays calm on the other side, looking like the leader I remember in the final stages of war. She's *every bit* a Renn:

wise, assured and blessed with unique magical gifts we're going to need on a new journey.

"When the white feather Oweyna released falls through the chasm, we jump together," Kaira says, causing me to look up at our Williynx ... wings spread to form a protective wall around us.

"Here we go," Kaira adds as the white feather rises from the mountain top, spinning into the chasm: the signal for us to jump into a star-filled abyss.

OUR FREE FALL FEELS *A LOT* DIFFERENT WITHOUT THE Williynx flying close by. There's no flight charm to guide us either, Kaira making it clear the magic in the mountains is enough. I've never had a reason to doubt my best friend until we get *dangerously* close to the surface, flying past Sylvian Creswell who raises a hand as we pass.

He looks as calm as Kaira, watching us dart towards the rugged floor of the mountainside until a blanket of stars wraps around us all, powered by the energy of the twisting, purple light flooding in.

Conrad takes a deep breath as we're spun towards the green-robed figure of Sylvian Creswell, tall and imposing in the tradition of all grand wizards. I shoot a glance to the mountain top, happy to see Laieya resting with her feathered comrades. So far, so good ... the feeling of being spun by a blanket of light and stars reminding me of the death ritual in The Cendryll.

Why I'm linking this new adventure to death isn't something I want to think about now, deciding it's an obvious association to make. After all, I watched the Quij wrap

Smyck in a multi-coloured blanket of colour, cocooning him forever with a touch of love.

Love is the thing I feel now, spinning alongside Conrad and Kaira as I try to control my racing mind. Whatever's in store for me in the sky realms, I'm ready for ... magic, mystery and mayhem etched in my skin ... scars that mark me as a strange breed in a spectacular world.

"We haven't got long before the chasm closes," Sylvian Creswell offers in welcome.

We're on the edge of the star-filled interior now, standing alongside our guide for the evening.

"I'll be brief in my explanation," Sylvian continues, lifting his green robe as he shifts position. "Kaira has work to do with our comrades above."

"The Winter King," I say.

"Yes, Guppy. Thylas Renn is a rare warrior offering passage to benefit us all."

"Stopping Taeia before he causes havoc, you mean," Conrad adds, glancing up at the imposing figure who looks regal in his green robe.

"Indeed, Conrad. Taeia's destiny as the future Winter King is not in question. What is yet to be determined is *when* and *how*. When will he reign and how will this come about?"

"So, where do we fit into this?" I ask, impatient to blast into the skies.

"Night Rangers transition to sky soldiers over time, Guppy, meaning you need to learn the art of studying the stars."

"It doesn't sound like we've got a choice," Conrad comments, touching the scar on his neck: a sign he's on edge.

"Everything is a choice, Conrad. You have the choice to

be a Night Ranger forever or travel beyond your current limitations."

"I'm in," I say.

"You want to walk into another war, Guppy?" Conrad challenges, buttoning his grey coat as the wind lifts.

"Who said anything about a war?"

"Well, let's see, Taeia's going to be The Winter King; the current Winter King is weakening with Bloodseekers closing in, and the sky realms don't seem to be getting along that well. Sounds like a war to me."

"Mediation is the current aim," Kaira states, interrupting our little battle.

"So, war *isn't* an option?" Conrad challenges.

"War is always an option, Conrad, but it's not on the horizon as we speak. Peaceful transition is the aim, maintaining balance between interconnected, magical worlds. What happens in the sky realms won't directly affect us but, as I said in The Cendryll earlier, once Taeia's in power he could cause problems for both realms."

"But if The Devenant isn't under threat, why should we risk our lives again?"

"Because the sky urchins, Williynx and Quliy have saved ours multiple times," I counter, getting a little annoyed with a hidden selfish streak in Conrad. "You want to leave our comrades to their fate when they're potentially in danger? Where do you think that's going to lead?"

"It's not our problem, Guppy."

"Well, I'm *making it* my problem; that's what a Society soldier does."

"Questions and choices for later," Sylvian states, blowing on the stars floating closest to him. "When you've made your choice, the following things must be considered: Night

Ranging will inevitably lead you back to Zilom and The Royisin Heights."

"Why?" Conrad challenges.

"Because malevs in hiding continue to seek passage to the sky realms. Many scattered after the battle with Erent Koll, moving further beyond The Society Sphere, hoping to evade capture. One particular sky realm — Kelph — runs a pirate economy offering refuge to the desperate: a refuge Alice Aradel tried to reach."

"The reason she appeared in The Shallows," I say, realising how our worlds are connected. All questionable movements link to the sky realms — not just Taeia's destiny but the channel used by the wild and wayward to evade capture. "So, Odin and Neve were trying to access the sky realms," I add, "meaning they're linked to all this."

"Yes," Kaira replies. "Flight is the temptation on offer for Domitus: a way of assessing which soldiers we can still trust in Drandok."

"Sounds like things are still fragile in the S.P.M.A." Conrad comments, looking a little less tense as the scales fall from his eyes. Night Ranging keeps a lid on bigger things happening around us, sort of keeping us in a loop of surveillance. I'm not a fan of going around in circles myself, so breaking the loop and keeping things calm in the sky realms makes sense to me.

"Stabilising the sky realms will help us all," Sylvian adds as he adjusts his green robe again, exposing his bare feet. "Hopefully, we've painted a picture of a challenge we either engage with or ignore. The Winter King is the beginning of this challenge; Taeia Renn's reign will be its conclusion."

"And there's no way of stopping Taeia becoming The Winter King?" Conrad poses, looking like he already knows the answer.

"Fate has a way of calling the Renns," Kaira adds, reaching for the white feather hovering nearby. "The chasm will start to close once the feather's in my hand. Follow Sylvian's path to the top."

"Where are you going?" I question, getting the sinking feeling my friend's returns will always be this brief.

"To continue building a path for us up there," Kaira replies, pointing to the triangle forming in the star-filled sky. "White Williynx only exist in the realm of The Winter King. Thylas Renn sent it to my dad as a way of testing Taeia. They both knew he'd fail — the reason my dad refused to train him. We're in a different phase now, chasing fate as it propels a relative towards a destiny certain to overwhelm him."

"Feels like history repeating itself," I say, watching as Kaira catches the white feather in her hand.

"In a way," she replies, "although something tells me Taeia's more lost than lethal but only time will tell. The main difference is The Devenant isn't at risk, meaning the S.P.M.A. is safe."

"So, it's more of a rescue mission," Conrad comments, looking up at Oweyna as the white Williynx flaps its wings, ready to take flight.

"A perfect way of putting it, Conrad," Kaira replies as a blanket of stars forms around her once more. "It's up to you whether you want to be part of it ... and Lucy and Noah, of course. I'll be back soon, sampling the sweets in Wimples and the milkshakes in Merrymopes."

"Say hello to The Winter King for me," I joke, smiling as Kaira steps off the mountain ledge, putting her hands together like a monk in prayer as the stars lift her upwards.

It's a comical gesture that gets a laugh from Conrad and me, waiting for Sylvian to guide us forwards. He does soon afterwards, tapping the rock face to send another shudder reverberating around us.

"Are you sure we're going to get out?" Conrad asks, looking a little worried as the chasm starts to close.

"I suggest you hold on to something," Sylvian replies with a strange smile ... his long, dark hair lifting as we rise suddenly ... the mountain ledge we're perched on jolting upwards as I grab on to Conrad, almost sending us both flying into the star-filled abyss.

Luckily, Conrad has the speed of thought to enact the Magneia charm, forming enough of a bond to keep us close to the mountain face as we rise at speed. Our platform of rock blasts upwards, racing to catch Kaira who offers a wave before she jumps onto Oweyna ... and then she's off ... a vision of white blasting into the evening sky.

28

THE COMFORT OF LOVE

The Cendryll skylight looks different from the outside, the beam of light it sends out over Society Square reminding me of a lighthouse. It was Jacob's idea to meet up here when he got wind of our return: a more discreet place to discuss all things Kaira.

After all, our heads are spinning because of our friend: a sudden return starting another whirlwind of adventure. It feels different compared to two years ago when we had no idea what was going on. This time, we're at the front and centre of things, the adults keeping their distance as we outgrow the need for supervision.

Casper and Philomeena's involvement will become clearer in time, facing the dilemma of helping a distant relative in the skies and a closer family tie in their midst.

None of us need to follow Kaira into the sky realms, but we all will. We're bound by something special so now it's a case of prepare our next move. Kaira's explained that Conrad and I need to get to know Sianna Follygrin and Aarav Khan better, leaving Jacob to train Taeia at rapid speed: an education that looks different now.

With the soft light beaming out across Society Square, I sit between my brother and Conrad on top of The Cendryll's skylight, wondering where I'm going to be two years from now. Hopefully, I'm still alive, discovering new realms in a magical universe that seems to go on forever. As long as Conrad, Kaira and Jacob are around, I'll be happy with that.

Our Williynx have left us for the evening, returning to their own journeys in the star-filled sky. As they fly away, I take out my Follygrin, hoping to track Kaira's movements but, of course, she's vanished beyond The Society Sphere ... her penchant's powers fading as she enters the realm of The Winter King. We'll be together again soon, learning the ways of the sky realms in time to prepare for whatever fate's got in store for us.

"So, you definitely want to go?" Jacob asks, sitting cross-legged alongside me as The Cendryll's skylight arcs left, lighting up Founders' Quad.

"Yep," I reply, rubbing dust off my black, leather trousers. "I'm not leaving Kaira out there on her own."

"I doubt she's on her own, Guppy."

"Well, I'm going to be alongside her when she's ready."

"First, we need to learn to read the stars," Conrad adds, offering me a conciliatory smile, "meaning more trips out to see Sianna in The Royisin Heights, and Aarav in Zilom."

"Lessons for us all then," Jacob says, looking up at the sky.

He'll always be the big brother looking out for us all, no matter how old we get. It's in his nature to protect and he's going to need every ounce of patience to keep a certain student in check.

"We'll help you with Taeia," I offer, "and the rest of the class, of course."

"He's going to cause problems," Jacob replies. "Some of the other students are already gravitating towards him."

"Let me guess: Katie and Ethan," I add.

"Yep."

"We'll keep an eye on them," Conrad comments, reaching out to hold my hand.

It's more a gesture of apology than romance, my boy wizard wanting to confirm his allegiance to the cause. I understand why Conrad hesitated — anything triggering his dad's death bringing up traumatic memories. Night Ranging is a relatively safe choice, after all, engaging with familiar faces to make sure they don't hover too close to criminal acts.

The path Kaira's been on is clearly a more dangerous one, but one I'm going to jump as soon as I'm called on. It's her family in the firing line again: Thylas Renn's reign as The Winter King coming to an end with a distant relative remaining blind to his destiny.

"Taeia's eighteen in less than six months," Jacob states, "meaning things are going to move quickly. So much for a quiet life in The Cendryll."

"You miss it, deep down," I reply, closing my Follygrin. "The magic and mayhem."

"Sometimes ... although the comfort of peace shouldn't be underestimated, Guppy."

"Peace is what we're trying to maintain again, only this time *up there*."

"Let's just hope Kaira knows what she's doing," Conrad adds, trying to find the triangle of fragile allegiance in the stars.

"She knows exactly what she's doing," I reply, wondering when I'll see my friend again.

"It's peaceful out here," Jacob comments, following the

light beaming out from The Cendryll. "I come out here a lot after lessons have finished. It reminds me of where it all began — in Founders' Quad — which seems like a lifetime ago now."

"Do you miss the above-ground world?" Conrad asks my brother.

Jacob shakes his head, running his right hand over the skylight we're perched on. "There's nothing there for me now. My world is here in the S.P.M.A. wherever that takes me."

"It's going to take you *on*," I reply, offering a smile to a brother who's always there when it matters most, and Conrad whose touch makes everything better.

As The Cendryll's skylight washes Society Square with a protective light, I glance up at the starlit sky once more, secretly wishing Kaira safe passage, preparing to embark on a new adventure in the skies. Two years of peace has allowed for healing in different forms, from scars to grief. It's also allowed time for love to blossom: a rare quality we're going to need again on our new adventures.

Lucy and Noah will be brought up to speed soon enough, but now it's time to enjoy a moment of peace on top of The Cendryll, feeling the warm glow of the skylight on my legs, thankful my best friend has returned in one piece soon to reveal magical realms hidden in the stars.

We'll be up there with her soon enough, meeting kings and battling Bloodseekers on our way to understanding the fragile balance in the sky realms: a balance ultimately resting in the hands of a lost boy destined for greatness.

TEASER CHAPTER BOOK 3

The top floor of Zucklewick's is as homely as I remember —
a log fire keeping us warm as we ponder the changing tide
in the skies. Zucklewick's is the Society bookshop situated in
Founders' Quad, catering for the above-ground world and
the magical one.

A particular charm reveals magical secrets hidden
within ordinary looking books. The four of us have met on
the top floor to go over recent events, including Kaira's
return and how it links to the mysteries in the sky.

There's also the question of Taeia's training, Casper hoping that attaching the lost boy to Jacob will tame the darkness in him. It won't be long before Taeia reaches the official wizarding age of eighteen when he'll be able to travel wherever he pleases, including to the sky realms.

His use of a mixed charm laced with a curse means his penchant stone has dimmed: a sign he's close to being shut out from the magical travel gifted to Society members. The only reason he can still access Periums is the S.P.M.A.'s authorisation of certain charms laced with dark magic — one of the changes after the last war.

We learnt the hard way that ignoring Gorrah (dark magic) has its downsides, particularly when you're dodging curses on the battlefield. Now, it's a case of delicate engagement where necessary, including the Domitus' use of a mild curse in their taming of the Silverbacks. Pure Gorrah ends your days in the S.P.M.A. so Taeia's lucky he's only had a taste of the destructive power of dark magic.

All Society soldiers have been trained in the use of certain mixed charms, the dangers of fighting blind a legacy left by the legendary Isiah Renn. It's fair to say the Renn family are at the heart of the magical world I call home, Casper and Philomeena overseeing all things in The Cendryll, Kaira returning to the sky realms to prepare a transition of power between Thylas Renn and his heir apparent: Taeia.

He's currently getting a taste of grand wizardry from the uncle who's agreed to train him, more for self-preservation than anything else. With the bad news sinking in that Taeia's the heir to The Winter King, certain plans have been put in motion, including keeping a close watch over his behaviour in The Cendryll: his new home after Jacob came to his rescue on The Hallowed Lawn.

Facing down a furious, white Williynx is no one's idea of fun, and the only reason Taeia's still alive is the compassion the Renns are famous for. I just hope he finds that same quality in himself before it's too late, or we'll have another battle in the skies.

Night Ranging is a perfect role for me, allowing me to discover new realms whilst keeping an eye over familiar ones, but there's something magnetic about mysteries engulfing the S.P.M.A. — the new one lying in the fragile triangle of allegiance I can finally locate in the stars. Now it's time for questions and preparations, though, Lucy and Noah coming to terms with a sudden change to our Night Ranging routine.

They're annoyed they can't travel to the sky realms until they've received more advanced training, arguing they're as equipped as we are for battle. It takes patience and a lot of persuasion to convince them otherwise: a delicate balance between reassurance and acceptance. Kaira's suggested the need for more training and since she's only one of us who's travelled to the sky realms, it makes sense to heed her advice.

Lucy and Noah are brilliant Night Ranger companions but they haven't faced fierce battle, something certain Society elders will prepare them for. Hopefully, it won't come to that but they understand the need to prepare for all eventualities.

Farraday's busy dealing with Taeia's old crew who are staying in The Cendryll, awaiting a decision about their futures. It's fair to say that Fillian, Mae and Alice's Night Ranging days are over, although whether that means a return to the above-ground world is yet to be seen.

Conrad and I are sitting near the fire, offering all the details we've got about Kaira's visit and where this is likely to lead us. Noah and Lucy are sitting in the armchairs on either side of the coffee table. It's where Ivo Zucklewick comes to relax when he gets the chance, the bookshop having a direct link to the Society library known as The Pancithon. Ivo's a night owl so is usually found roaming the Pancithon at night, catching sleep between customers searching for rare books.

I listen to Ivo below, opening up Zucklewick's to the keen shoppers waiting outside. Founders' Quad comes alive soon afterwards, another busy day for the members who run the above ground establishments. Along with keeping a pristine bookshop, Ivo is also a master of subtle magic, suggesting a Blindman's Watch might come in handy with Taeia's arrival in The Cendryll.

It's a pamphlet acting as a surveillance device; you tuck into a book near the location of the person you're tracking, opening the pamphlet up to reveal all. The books are housed high up in The Cendryll, beneath the skylight, but Jacob's got a plan to carry a book on him from now on, leaving it in the room he's using for his lessons. It won't be long before Taeia influences the younger students, and the magical pamphlet will pick up anything suspicious.

"So, we stick to Night Ranging while you have all the fun in the sky realms?" Noah queries, playing with the buttons on his waistcoat.

He's clearly not pleased that he and Lucy have been side lined temporarily, although I remind him again that it's Kaira's orders.

"We won't be going anywhere until Kaira returns," I explain, putting another log on the fire. "The Night Ranging continues as normal until we've got a clear path to the skies."

"To The Winter King," Lucy adds, seeming to have taken the news better than Noah.

"Right."

"And how long's our training going to take?" Noah prompts.

"Until the Society elders are happy you're equipped for whatever's ahead of us," Conrad replies, sitting cross legged alongside me. "Hopefully, it's more of an adventure than anything else but meeting Sianna Follygrin and Aarav Khan weren't coincidences: the two people likely to prepare us for the skies. Whatever's going on up there is likely to involve a degree of danger."

"Danger we should be walking into?" Noah challenges.

"Danger we choose to walk into," I reply as the fire crackles. "Night Ranging's our official role; the sky realms are a choice. If it means helping a Winter King in need, leading to things staying calm in the skies and down here, I'm in."

"When do you think Kaira will be back?" Lucy asks, holding out her arms to feel the warmth of the fire.

"Soon," I say, feeling a familiar rhythm building with an old friend. "Until then, we help Jacob during the day and keep an eye on things at night."

"I'm not sure I'm ready to step onto a battlefield?" Lucy adds, her right foot tapping nervously. "Monitoring malevs is one thing, but going to battle with Bloodseekers ... I don't know if I'm cut out for that."

"Only one way to find out," Noah replies, offering Lucy a reassuring smile. "Return to Zilom and The Royisin Heights to learn from the best. My uncle rubs me up the wrong way but there's no doubting his magical abilities, and he's a sky soldier meaning he's perfectly placed to prepare us."

"And Sianna will hopefully tell us more about what her

unofficial role is," Conrad adds, "studying the stained-glass floor and shifting visions in the broken glass. Looks like she hasn't hung up her wand yet."

"We've got time to make up our minds before Kaira returns," I add, standing with Conrad and heading over to the window to look over Founders' Quad. "Whether to stay here or travel to the skies."

I study busy streets, my mind already made up. When Kaira returns, I'll head to the sky realms with her, ready to meet a fading Winter King and the Bloodseekers closing in on his white fortress. As the streets of Founders' Quad fill with customers returning to their favourite shops, I think about the incredible journey I've been on ... from magical sweets to menacing Melackin and a battle to the death in shifting sands.

New adventures are on the horizon now, hovering in the sky realms: a brooding, hidden world of wonder ready to reveal its mysteries. Conrad appears alongside me, offering me a smile. He's come round to the idea of defending comrades not directly linked to us, remembering those who came to our aid: sky urchins, ageing giants and Society legends risking their lives to protect ours.

The tables are turned now, the youngest wizards flying to the aid of a fading one: beauty and unity at the heart of everything we do.

"Ready to travel to the unknown again?" Conrad asks as he takes my hand.

He's dressed in jeans and a white T-shirt, the scar running along his neck a mark of his bravery and sacrifice. My scars are lighter, marking my arms and legs and I'm sure I'll acquire more soon enough.

"It's what we do best," I reply, studying the green eyes

that lack the concern they previously had. "We've got pretty good at navigating our way through trouble."

"It was nice to have some peace and quiet for a while, allowing us to have some fun in the skies."

"We can still have some fun," I say, stepping closer to my boy wizard, "we just might have to dodge a few Bloodseekers along the way."

"Sounds like paradise," Conrad jokes, the squeeze of his hand signalling he's committed to the journey ahead.

"I say we fly to Zilom later," I add, stepping away from the window with Conrad. "Get up to speed with things happening in the sky realms. By the sound of things, Aarav's going to be our guide, preparing us for whatever's needed."

"Then onto Sianna in The Royisin Heights," Noah adds, seeming to have already made his decision. "The setup of her dwelling allows her to see the sky, meaning she's probably the best person to teach us how to read the stars. I don't know why that's going to matter but I think I will."

"Maybe the stars work like a Nivrium," Lucy suggests, getting up from the armchair to stand by the fire. "A Nivrium allows us to read water, helping us to judge the temperature of the Society. The stars marking the sky realms could do the same, assuming we can learn how to read them: flickering in certain patterns to show stability and danger."

"Brilliant, Lucy," Noah adds, running a hand through his long, dark hair.

"Brilliant indeed," I echo, wondering if Lucy's about to discover a lot more than battle charms in our new adventures.

"So, Zilom then The Royisin Heights," Conrad states. "Gather the information we need before Kaira returns."

We all nod in agreement before Noah adds, "Is there any

food up here?"

"I doubt Ivo would thank us for raiding his cupboards," I reply, "but Jacob makes a mean cooked breakfast."

"Hasn't he got to teach?"

"It's still early and he'll want to know our plan anyway. Come on, let's use Ivo's Scribberal to send Jacob a message, then back to The Cendryll for some breakfast.."

"What's it like?" Lucy asks as we prepare to leave via the door near the fire: a magical portal to take us on. "Battle, I mean."

"Like a brutal orchestra playing a perfect harmony," I reply, surprising myself with the response. "It's unforgettable and unforgivable at the same time, but we've got legends on our side and a unity that's hard to shatter. Don't worry, Lucy, if we run into battles you'll have all the preparation you need and loyal comrades alongside you."

"Well, I can't wait to meet some Bloodseekers," Noah offers with a smile, ducking as Lucy swipes at him.

They're a cute couple, finding their way in the romantic way of things as our magical universe revolves around us, preparing to send us spinning towards the stars.

Buy Book 3

ABOUT THE AUTHOR

I'm the author of the **Kaira Renn** series, **The Fire Witch Chronicles** and **Magic & Misdemeanours**, all set in The Society for the Preservation of Magical Artefacts. (S.P.M.A.)

If you enjoyed the book, please consider **leaving a review on Amazon.**

To receive updates and a chance to win free copies of future titles, sign up to my newsletter **here**.

You can also join my **Facebook group** dedicated the S.P.M.A. universe.

ALSO BY R.A. LINDO

THE S.P.M.A. UNIVERSE

5 books per series

Kaira Renn Series: origin series

The Fire Witch Chronicles: spin-off series one

Magic & Misdemeanours: spin-off series two

Printed in Great Britain
by Amazon